SPOOVES

A Collection of Short Humor

By Tim Miller

SPOOVES

Copyright © **2022 Tim Miller**

All rights reserved.

Published by **Gnatcatcher Press 2022**

San Marcos, CA, USA

No parts of this publication may be reproduced, stored in a retrieval system, or transmitted in any form or by any means, electronic, mechanical, photocopying, recording, or otherwise, without the prior written permission of the copyright owner.

This book is sold subject to the condition that it shall not, by way of trade or otherwise, be lent, resold, hired out, or otherwise circulated without the publisher's prior consent in any form of binding or cover other than that in which it is published and without a similar condition including this condition being imposed on the subsequent purchaser.

So Ben, you can't buy this and lend it to Marty. Not without my permission, anyway. I'll think about it.

Under no circumstances may any part of this book be photocopied for resale.

GP
GNATCATCHER
PRESS

spoof \spo͞of \ *noun* INFORMAL : a humorous imitation of something in which its characteristic features are exaggerated for comic effect. — n, pl **spoofs** also: **spooves** also: **spooveses**

Humor can be a relief, like an aspirin tablet.
-Kurt Vonnegut

Table of Contents

CURRENT RESIDENT

June 14, 2012

To: Catherine Fredricks, Managing Broker for Windmore
Real Estate

Hello Ms. Fredricks,

Would you please remove our address from your mailing
list? We receive frequent brochures from your company
and are not interested in your real estate services at this
time. Thank you.

Current Resident
1022 Holiday Rd.
San Marcos, WA 92078

July 21, 2012

Dear Catherine Fredricks,

Can you please remove my address from your mailing list
(second request)? 1022 Holiday Rd. San Marcos, WA
92078. Would like to be environmentally friendly. If you've
already done so, disregard this message.

Thank you.

August 28, 2012

Hello,

This is my third attempt to be removed from your mailing list. Mr. & Mrs. Haaland no longer live at this address and I'd appreciate a reduction in my junk mail. Thank you.

Current Resident
1022 Holiday Rd.
San Marcos, WA 92078

September 20, 2012

Dear Madam,

Can you remove the following address from your mailing list?

Mr. and Mrs. Haaland Or Current Resident
1022 Holiday Rd.
San Marcos, WA 92078

The frequent mailings are arriving in San Marcos, CA. We are not in the least bit interested in your real estate services. Thank you. (This is my fourth request.)

October 9, 2012

Catherine,

I'm taking time out of my day to once again request that you no longer send real estate brochures to 1022 Holiday Rd. San Marcos, WA 92078. I understand that you are in the business of recruiting clients, but I am not looking to buy or sell in the foreseeable future. (Besides, even if I was, I already have a real estate agent that I'm comfortable with.) Please, reduce the amount of paper your company uses, go green, and take my address off your mailing list. Thank you!

Current Resident

November 15, 2012

Dear Irresponsible Business Leader,

You have blatantly ignored my repeated requests to get off your mailing list. I have no intentions of hiring your company for any real estate needs.

For one thing, you can't honor a simple request to reduce the number of trees you murder in Washington by sending off these brochures all over God knows where. Also, for a real estate broker, I'd think you'd be better at geography. There is no San Marcos in Washington.

I don't mean to rant here, it's just that I'm frustrated because every month I have to toss your brochure, with your smiling face, into the recycling bin needlessly. It's very wasteful.

I understand junk mail, and businesses trying to reach more customers through advertisements in the mail. I know the economy is tough and advertising needs to be proactive—even aggressive. Businesses are not to blame, especially if the method is proven to work.

When I saw that you are based in Seattle, Washington, and were mailing brochures to an address that doesn't exist, in San Marcos, Washington, I thought I would take a moment out of my day to alert you to this error so that you could correct it and thus reduce the impact your business has on the environment. I thought I would do the Earth a small favor. Every piece of paper counts.

I have tried repeatedly. Since you've been ignoring me, I've continued my attempts on principle. In fact, this is my sixth try! And the brochures keep coming. So I thought I would once more appeal to your humanity and our common ground of being current residents of Earth:

Please, save some paper and remove our address from your mailing list.

Current Resident
1022 Holiday Rd.
San Marcos, WA 92078
Planet Earth

December 23, 2012

Yo Cath,

What a fucking surprise! I opened my mailbox and saw your dumb smiling face again. Oh joy! Another Home Update installment from the Windmore Real Estate Company. Once again, I rush indoors, tingling with excitement over volume 33106. It's almost unfair that I've had to wait an entire month since volume 33105. Your enthralling market updates and precision pricing guides practically float in my dreams. The last issue has been the most insightful real estate brochure I've ever read. I've been anxiously waiting to see if you could repeat, nay, even top such exquisite writing.

Breathless with anticipation, I rip open the brochure and turn as always to your eloquent, comforting, and sage "Things To Consider" section.

I have a Thing for you To Consider: You're a whore bag!

I'm sure if I emailed you with a request for real estate assistance you'd respond in a heartbeat, wouldn't you? That's because you're a selfish bitch. Who cares that the world's forests are shrinking, as long as Catherine Fredricks has real estate business? It's unreal how completely out of touch with reality and self-indulgent some people can be. Not to mention negligent.

You are wasting time, energy, and resources sending these stupid, inane brochures to San Marcos, California, and you probably don't even realize it. No time to think of the postal worker who has to carry one more useless piece of paper, or the sanitation worker who has to lift my recycling bin. Well, why would you, if you have a healthy bottom line? No time for details when you have taxes to evade and vacations to plan. Shocking, the incompetence and sheer disregard of Corporate America!

Honestly, how much makeup do you need for your photograph? And that haircut makes you look like a little boy with wrinkles. That's right: Benjamin Button, the real estate agent.

I could give two shits that your son Aaron will be joining you as your business partner. Great, more nepotism in America! Once again, a more qualified applicant is kicked to the curb because baby boy spent his college years getting shit-faced. Come work for mommy! In a few years you can make partner. It's disgusting.

What's that? You and Nepotism Boy have been chosen by industry experts as one of Seattle Magazine's Five Star Real Estate Agents, the top 5% of real estate agents in the Seattle area? That doesn't speak very well of the overall intelligence of the Seattle real estate industry, considering that you mail brochures to a town that doesn't exist—in California! Basically, you're saying 95% of Seattle real estate agents can't find California on a fucking map. Unbelievable.

Oh, and I'm not buying that whole Community Service Day bullcrap on the back page. Every year your company joins together to complete neighborhood improvement projects? What a lark! That picture of a lady raking leaves is a fucking insult to people who really do try to make a difference on this Earth, even small ones like reducing junk mail.

Whose lawn is she raking, Aaron's?

I almost vomited when I actually read your closing sentence. "An investment in our neighborhoods gives us all a better place to call home." Does that include the make-believe ones like San Marcos, Washington, or do you consider pollution and waste in real communities like San Marcos, California, to be an *investment*?

Go ahead, keep mailing me your dumbass brochures with your arrogant smile, and I'll keep recycling them, because what difference does it make? Just keep smiling and murdering the Earth!

Does anything we do really matter in the grand scheme of the universe, anyway?

Current Resident
1022 Holiday Rd.
San Marcos, WA 92078

I was in the middle of reading when he walked in for the first time. It was early January. He hovered out of the corner of my eye as I reached a critical turning point in my novella—the protagonist three-putting the fifteenth green.

When I finished I looked over to see a tall, skinny white guy wearing all black: baggy jeans sagging below his waist, a T-shirt three sizes too big, and a do-rag wrapped around his head. He sat down across from me and I noticed he had tattoos on his fingers that, if I had to guess, were symbols for a gang.

Richard, the group's facilitator and author of the currently unpublished memoir *The Perilous Path to Christ*— as he always does on fresh faces— pounced like a leopard from a tree.

"This is the Riverview Writers Group. Are you a writer?"

"Sort of."

"What's your name?" Marsha asked. A retired teacher, she was halfway through writing her first novel. The protagonist befriends a transgender classmate at a design school and there is something going on with green gunk.

"Q-tip," he said, staring at nothing.

Richard explained the group's protocol in the exact manner he had described it to me three months earlier. Q-tip played with his tongue ring. Then it was time for the group to give me feedback, and—likely the result of our newest member—the dramatic and pivotal twist in my story was lost on everyone. When the circle was complete, it was my turn to respond.

"I ask you, my fellow writers, did anyone notice how my character *had not once* three-putted in the whole story?" I began to list the other obvious signs of my kairotic moment, but the word *kairotic* proved to be a snag. Woody started in on its Greek origins and, before I knew it, the timer on Richard's phone beeped and everyone's attention shifted to Q-tip to see if he had pages.

He didn't. Well, I thought, at least he brings an element of diversity to the group; no one else was under sixty.

Whenever his turn to offer feedback came around, he whispered, "Pass," except when Debbie read her my-dead-son's-birthday essay.

"I love your writing," he said in a soft voice. "It's achingly beautiful." I remember distinctly he said *achingly*.

We didn't see him for a month. When he came back, again he would whisper "pass" each time it was his turn to give feedback, and only commented on Debbie's waking-up-with-grief essay. "I loved it," he said. He didn't seem too impressed with my golf fiction.

Q-tip showed up once a month. He never brought any writing. One time I went to the bathroom to find a drug bust going down—not all that unusual considering the location of the library near the public transit center. I thought maybe Q-tip ducked into our writer's group as a way to avoid Five-O attention, though I didn't share this with anyone in the group.

In April, Richard said, "Q-tip, we enjoy your company. But to be an active member you need to bring in your own work."

We didn't see him for another month. Then last Tuesday he walked in with a stack of wrinkled pages. He had scrawled by hand with a smudgy ballpoint pen and somehow managed to find a photocopier.

Devon, the group secretary (and the real authority figure), asked him for his word count.

"Three-oh-nine," he said in his soft voice.

His count was the lowest, even shorter than Clive's flash fiction, so he went first. You almost couldn't hear him.

the ball gos thru. the bears have beet the eagles 18-16. ther movin on to the devishunal round. the players cary u off the field thats when u hear broken glass. cuz im comin fo yo ass

yur dreamin. the ball didnt go through no uprights. it double doinked. just like the four doinks against the lions in november

then u hear me killin yur dog. yur dog that dont care about the bears and still loves u. he be barkin. dont kill me dont me. u aint gonna know what hit me

then he hear me on the stairs. i clime loudly with my steal toe boots. im comin to kill yur ass. but first i gonna kill yur wife. she dont care what happens to the bears but she gon care plenti when i kick her pretty bitch ass. she gonna be like no no but i gonna be like yes yes. dum bitch gonna be fraid. he gonna hold her head while i kick it 43 yards right down the middle.

she gonna be like why

The standard minute passed while everyone made notes. When Richard's phone timer beeped it was Jack's turn to share his thoughts, since he was sitting to Q-tip's right.

"I'll start," said the retired lawyer and author of a legal thriller (in progress) called *The Dove's Shadow*. "There's some very strong emotion in this piece. I'm often told that my work lacks emotion, so that's a real strong point for you. That's all I have to say."

Clive, a South African grammarian, went next. He didn't even get through the difference between proper and common nouns before Richard's phone beeped. Next was Wanda, a cozy mystery writer.

"I thought this was very interesting," she began, as usual. "The overall voice serves your purpose. There are a few words, like 'break' and 'steel,' that are tricky and get all of us from time to time, so I've made notes. Nice job. Gary."

"The dream sequence that starts it off," said Gary, the author of some Asimovian sci-fi. "That's gotta go. It's a cliché. When you're trying to hook your reader, what you're really doing is establishing trust. And starting with a dream does the opposite. Devon."

The author of an unpublished YA novel called *The Curse of Love*, Devon started with her typical phrase: "So I agree with everyone so far." I knew what she was going to say next. I thought there was a chance she might not, but deep down, I knew she would. "You have an *-ly* word that needs to be cut. The killer climbed the stairs *loudly*. We don't need loudly. Just say 'I climbed the stairs.' But overall good job."

Next was Woody, the science blogger. "About half these words you don't need," he said, like always. He harped on the run-on sentence at the end. "We don't need to know the last time they won a playoff game." Then he closed with his usual note of ambiguity. "Otherwise, it's going somewhere."

After Woody was Marsha.

"There are some issues with point of view," she said. "We get a little lost in the pronouns. For example, 'you ain't gonna know what hit me.' Is that the dog's POV? I think it should stay with what the kicker hears. Also, 'she gonna be like why' needs a question mark. Richard."

Our facilitator sighed. "When you first started reading, I thought, what kind of lunatic threatens the life of a professional football kicker? For missing a kick and losing a game. For being flawed and human as our creator has made all of us."

He squinted pensively out the window. "Thou shalt not kill."

Then he gazed upward. "But I noticed you taking notes during the feedback. So now I'm thinking this is one of God's children, contemplating an eternal sin, who also cares about becoming a better writer." Richard directed his gleaming eyes at Q-tip. "That last part," he said, and paused with one of his pregnant silences. "That, at least, is to be commended."

Then it was my turn.

"Pass," I said. After all, he never said one word about my golf stories.

HUMANIZE MAYBE

Not all that long ago, I attended a professional development session at my school. The purpose of the training was to address the following question: What should you do in the event of an active shooter?

Nothing is remotely funny or humorous about active shooters or the reality that public schools need to train their employees for the potential of such an event.

However. There was something that I did, in fact, find humorous during the training. Which is sort of what I do when life turns lugubrious. Here it is.

The PowerPoint presentation, from the San Diego County Office of Education in cooperation with the Department of Homeland Security, included a slide with the following table.

Trying to Humanize Yourself with an Assailant

Armed Robbery	Yes
Homicide	Maybe
Active Shooter	No

I would like to focus on the Homicide Maybe row for the following short play.

<u>HUMANIZE MAYBE</u>

(Scene: a dark alley in an American city. A FATHER OF THREE has gone out to get a quart of milk so that his children will have milk for breakfast, but since this father is not familiar with the city, let's say it's Baltimore—he's there for his sister's wedding— with a lot of brick buildings which can be confusing—but it's not Baltimore as the author does not wish to imply that a lot of murders or robberies happen in Baltimore. This FATHER OF THREE

is using his phone's Maps app and not understanding why it keeps buzzing to alert him that he is walking in the wrong direction. The FATHER OF THREE, head down, staring at his phone, mistakenly turns down a dark alley and then pauses as his phone vibrates and redirects him yet again. Suddenly an ASSAILANT jumps out from behind a dumpster and holds something that feels like a gun to his back.)

ASSAILANT
Don't move, or I'll kill you. Give me all your money.

FATHER OF THREE
OK! OK! Don't shoot! *(Puts hands in the air.)* Hey, can I ask you one real quick question?

ASSAILANT
Huh? All right—but just one. Any tricks and you're a goner.

FATHER OF THREE
Would it help if I humanize myself?

ASSAILANT
What does 'humanize' mean?

FATHER OF THREE
You know, like make you realize that I'm a human being. That this quart of milk is for my little kids, three girls all under six. That I have a family and a job and that I like to eat salami and play guitar and root for the Cubs. You know, that other people would kinda miss me if you killed me. And my school would have to find a new science teacher. I would miss my sister's wedding. Well, weddings. See, it's the first of two weddings—it's a long story. That kinda stuff.

ASSAILANT

I didn't know you could just add *-ize* to the end of a word. Is that a verb now?

FATHER OF THREE

I believe it is. To make human. Like if you weaponize something, say, a stapler, then you are making it a weapon. That's probably not a good example. Demonize is to make a demon. Like the press is demonizing Donald Trump. That might not be a good example either. Are you a Republican? Or, I guess the right question is, Did you vote for Trump? Not that it's either here or there. Politics are so crazy right now. I mean you can be a Republican and totally against Trump. Not that it's any of my business. You might not even have voted. Though you really should vote. Listen to me, just rambling.

ASSAILANT

Shut up. Give me some money or you're dead.

FATHER OF THREE

Wait! I have just one more, like, real real quick question.

ASSAILANT

(Grumbling) Aaargh! Fine. Last question. Then you die. And don't get off subject.

FATHER OF THREE

Is this a robbery or would you consider it a homicide?

ASSAILANT

Why do you ask?

FATHER OF THREE

See, I'm a teacher—more humanizing here—and I recently went through a training about what to do in the event of a public shooting. I know. Crazy times we live in. Don't get me started on the whole arming teachers debate. Anyway, there was this slide about how you shouldn't ever try to humanize yourself to an active shooter.

ASSAILANT

Makes sense.

FATHER OF THREE

Right? But there was this table about how, in the event of an armed robbery, you should. Right next to ARMED ROBBERY it said YES.

ASSAILANT

I could see that. An armed robber doesn't necessarily want to kill people, but he—or she—will if they have to, to get what they're after.

FATHER OF THREE

Exactly. I knew from the moment you held me against my will that you were a reasonable person. *(FATHER OF THREE starts to turn to face ASSAILANT, but is prevented with gun-like object.)* But next to HOMICIDE the table said MAYBE. So then I was trying to think of examples of when you would try to humanize yourself before someone trying to murder you and when you wouldn't. Unfortunately, there wasn't another slide. I guess it would have been off topic.

ASSAILANT

Hmmm ... I could see like a cheating husband situation, where it doesn't matter. Like the husband cheated and the wife is gonna kill him and there's nothing he could say. She knows he's a human, and a lousy one at that.

FATHER OF THREE

Bingo. I was thinking along those lines, like a big variable is whether the person trying to kill you knows you or not, because if they know you, then they already know you're a human.

ASSAILANT

Another very . . . um . . .

FATHER OF THREE

Variable.

ASSAILANT

Yeah, that. Thank you.

FATHER OF THREE

Don't mention it.

ASSAILANT

So, another very-uh-bull *(FATHER OF THREE nods.)* is probably whether the murder is premeditated or not. I can see how another slide is really wanting in the presentation.

FATHER OF THREE

Right? And why do they say 'premeditated'? Is it like you meditate beforehand about murdering someone? Ohhhhm. Kill Gary. Ohhhhhhm. Kill Gary. That would seem like an oxymoron.

ASSAILANT

I thought an oxymoron was like jumbo shrimp—Hey! Wait a minute. That was another question. Quit trying to change the subject. You're gonna die. *(ASSAILANT prods the object further into FATHER OF THREE's back.)*

FATHER OF THREE

(*Desperately*) Wait wait wait—at the beginning you asked for my money.

ASSAILANT

Oh yeah, I did, didn't I?

FATHER OF THREE

So isn't this a robbery? Not a homicide? And haven't I humanized myself sufficiently?

ASSAILANT

Well . . .

FATHER OF THREE

I have cash. And credit cards. And a phone that keeps vibrating for some reason. You can have it all. I won't cancel the cards for 24 hours.

ASSAILANT

Make it 48. And the milk, too. I'm thirsty as hell. Lay it all down slowly and walk away. Nothing sudden or it's the end.

FATHER OF THREE

(*Complies, very slowly and deliberately, setting down phone and wallet and milk. He takes about ten steps and then, without turning, says:*) Wait, was this an Armed Robbery Yes or a Homicide Maybe?

ASSAILANT

Homicide No. (*He fires.*)

Are you sick of preparing dinner night after night under government stay-at-home orders? Are you willing to trade a little taste and nutrition to feed your family's yap-holes and put everyone to bed already? Well, we've got just what you've been looking for!

During this worldwide pandemic, who has the time, money, or means to prepare wholesome, healthy meals every single night? We're talking every. Single. Night.

If you're out of ideas, you're in luck!

Introducing the new cookbook for frazzled parents, *Quick and Crappy*. You'll find all your favorite recipes, with minimal cost and maximum emphasis on getting everyone fed quickly so you can have that glass of wine and go to bed.

You'll find all the classics: Chili Mac, Sloppy Mess, Noodle Party, Creamy Cheesy, Meaty Casserole, Hamburger Ploppers, Hamdoggers, Hot Doggles, Cheesy Chicken, Ranchy Chicken, BBQ Sweet Chickers, PB & Yeah!, Ricey Beefy, Stir Crazy Stir Fry, Turkey Mess, Just Soup, Cracker Attacker, Tuna Toonie, and more! Of course, you'll also find plenty of microwavable platters that you can prepare in literally minutes. Throw in a piece of toast and put some baby carrots on the side and, *voilà*, dinner is served. No more expensive, time intensive, healthy meals that end up in the trash can.

Your family won't be too enthusiastic, but they won't starve either. Each meal is, after all, mostly edible food. And it's usually warm. They'll manage to choke down a few spoonfuls that will keep their tummies from rumbling until morning, so they can't complain too loudly, now can they? And usually there are—wait for it—leftovers! Lunch tomorrow? Done!

No more haggling over baby bites. To counteract potential complaining, we recommend serving sugary beverages like soda, sports drinks, or fruit punches that will help them gulp away the taste, or lack thereof, in their meal. If the complaining should become excessive, our cookbook comes with a list of *Quick and Crappy* desserts to bribe them with.

Though high in sodium, sugars, preservatives, processed foods, and fats, these meals are low in stress, headaches, ingredients, thought, effort, and, perhaps most importantly, dishes! No more pots and pans for dad! Go ahead, put your feet up! Have a beer and watch that game on TV! Even if it is from 1991 . . .

Dinner will no longer be a nightly obstacle or grudge match. If your kids don't like it, that means you can put them to bed even earlier. Take it from the authors, the myriad benefits of using this no-nonsense cookbook are too numerous to list. They just keep cropping up. Forget about risking your life at busy supermarkets for fresh produce. You can buy what you need in bulk, and cheaply, too. Dishes will no longer be a soul-sapping chore. We suggest paper plates and plastic forks. Worried about the environment? Use the time and money you've saved to plant a tree!

So quit washing those veggies and chopping whatever you're chopping. Crumple up that grocery list. Order a copy today and relax. Spend more time together as a family. Or not! The choice is yours.

Now you will have the luxury, thanks to *Quick and Crappy.*

Publisher's note: Some of the foods included in this book are not approved by the FDA. In fact, some of the foods might not be food. This book lacks any oversight from anyone with any real, actual knowledge of nutrition, basic science, or common sense for that matter. This book was made by two exhausted, run-down, burned-out parents at the end of their quarantine rope.

They don't really care about your family's well-being; they just want your money so they can use DoorDash more often. The publishers of *Quick and Crappy* strongly encourage you not to buy this book at all, even as a gag gift. We only published it because, well, it's a long story. Basically, it boils down to not reporting a car accident so insurance rates wouldn't be affected. If you have to buy this book and use it, we don't recommend eating these meals every night. Maybe once a month, on a Friday, some of the thirty-seven mac 'n' cheese options might be reasonable. The third one with hot dogs isn't too bad.

The publishers are hereby released from all liability stemming from purchase or use of *Quick and Crappy*. We are specifically not responsible for childhood obesity, chronic health problems (including dental), divorces, or children running away.

The Final Blog Entry from Desiree, Yoga Instructor on the Second Death Star

It's hard to believe we've been practicing for two years as of today! It's only appropriate to commemorate this anniversary by revisiting our amazing story. The Emperor had just arrived to personally oversee construction of the second Death Star when we got our start. It feels like only yesterday that he electrocuted the former chief weapons engineer . . .

Everyone was feeling the strain of conquering the galaxy: Stormtroopers were stiff from all that standing. Helmet data from across the Empire revealed chronic shallow breathing. TIE fighter pilots had poor circulation from sitting too much. Scout troopers had sore wrists and lower back pain from all those hours on speeder bikes. AT-AT drivers had issues in their cervical vertebrae from looking down. The heavy blasters wreaked havoc on snowtroopers' joints. When the inevitable construction delays occurred, stress amongst commanders went through the unfinished roof.

The Emperor was reluctant to allocate resources away from his weapons systems. But, amazingly, he finally conceded to Jon, the Royal Guard in charge of the Imperial Wellness program, and agreed to include a yoga studio in the Martial Arts Hall. He even permitted music. Classes were small at first, but word quickly spread. Some say it was the incentivized discount on health premiums, but I knew otherwise. We were providing something those vanquishing the galaxy in service to our Emperor were sorely lacking: mindfulness.

We started with one room, which we called the Asteroid Oasis. Pretty soon mats from all sectors of the Empire covered the floor. We even had a few bounty hunters pass through. We added a second room for hot yoga, called the Dagobah Den, and finally a third room, the Bespin Cloud.

Vader was the wild card. No one knew what he would do.

At first, he scoffed at the art of yoga and meditation. About six weeks after the studio opened, he walked in during a Slow Flow After Light Speed class and openly derided what he called our "Sith snake-charming class." Admiral Piett was in a chair position, and Vader knocked him right over using the Force. Then he pushed the rest of the class back against the wall, lifted all the blocks, rolled up all our mats, and said that yoga could never come near the power of the Dark Side. He turned and walked out, the blocks thudding on the floor. We didn't see him again the entire first year. But occasionally we felt him. He would knock over yogis in the middle of practice, send blocks across the room, or momentarily cut off the air supply of an instructor.

No one knows how or when the change happened. Some say losing his hand caused some wrist complications, and yoga positions such as downward dog are the perfect strength building remedy. Others say it was the toll of aging as a cyborg. Still others are convinced that, although the Force is certainly powerful and comes with mindfulness out the wazoo, it has little emphasis on the breath. Members of this camp point to a change in Lord Vader's audible breathing apparatus as support for their theory.

Whatever it was, Vader came marching into the Asteroid Oasis one morning for a Vinyasa class. He was capeless, wearing yoga attire and even sandals. (His yellow toenails caused quite a stir.) Glen was the instructor. The first twenty minutes were tense, but Vader moved through the positions. Then Glen made his fatal error. He offered hands-on assistance for a pigeon pose and Vader killed him. We all miss Glen very much.

We were all surprised when Vader showed up at the Cloud Room for Jon's Bootcamp. Everything was going fine, according to the stormtroopers that were in class that day, until the classic Sy Snootles song "Daddy Don't Preach" came on. Something about the song really irked Vader. Using the Force, he ripped the stereo out of the wall and smashed Jon's skull. The other members of the Royal Guard used their crimson yoga towels to soak up the pool of blood.

After that, all of us instructors were on edge. We all knew Vader could barge into any class and kill us right on our mats. We made a pledge then and there to commit to our practice, to bring balance and well-being to the Galactic Empire.

Vader disappeared for a while. The rumor was that he had decided to follow the cousin of that rebel scum Admiral Ackbar—some amphibious guru that practices *daya* (compassion for all creatures)—and did a deep dive into meditation on both his abandonment issues and the uncertainty of his identity.

Whatever it was, it worked. When he came back to the Death Star, he was a new Lord Vader. He showed up religiously at Matt's Wednesday night Hot Yoga in Cold Space class. Most Death Star yogis claim that it was Matt's laid-back style that drew Vader to the class. Others say it was his playlists that prominently featured Max Rebo's solo album "The Dark Side of Endor's Moon." Vader seemed as healthy as ever. Some claimed they could hear the ujjayi breath coming through his apparatus. One vice admiral reported that his torturing of rebel spies and incompetent commanders took a kinder, gentler turn.

For a while it was like clockwork, every Wednesday. Vader, Ackbar's cousin, and a random group of Bothans. Apparently this was a mutinous faction that had denounced the Bothan culture's focus on the pursuit of gaining power and influence. No one said anything because their arrival coincided with an Imperial survey showing a surge in tranquility. Productivity and oppression soared while the list of conquered territories continued to grow.

But the Bothans were a strange bunch, all right. One of them always pestered me in the hallway after my Restore Evil, Restore You class. He wanted to know if, as a weapons engineer, I had access to the Death Star's digital blueprints, which of course I do. He said Vader wanted to build his own studio. Finally, he said if I didn't give them to him, I would answer to Lord Vader himself. So I gave him a copy to get him to leave me alone. I doubt if anything will come of it.

Then there was a disturbance in the Force. Something about Vader's son and daughter, or maybe both. Trust me, I know—it's hard being a parent in the Empire. Suddenly Vader couldn't hold even the basic warrior poses. A TIE fighter pilot, lucky to survive, witnessed the whole thing from his baby cobra position. Right as "Any Galaxy You Like" came on, Vader collapsed while executing a chaturanga. He ripped off his sweat-resistant muscle tee and breathable sutra pants and stormed out of the studio. Desperate, Matt instructed the class to go to child's pose, but it was too late. Vader returned with his cape, which he never wore in the studio. He marched back into the Oasis with his boots on, and Matt must have known it was over. We all miss Matt very much.

Almost everyone in the class died, including Ackbar's cousin and most of the Bothans. Vader's sandals are still where he left them.

As I sit here on this Tuesday morning, sipping kombucha tea, preparing for my Sculpt and Destroy class, I'm mindful of where we've been. It is with profound gratitude that I take this time to reflect on the peace we've created in the heart of the galaxy's deadliest weapon. And now I turn the page, open to the possibilities of what lies ahead. Just yesterday, an AT-ST walker driver from Endor suggested that a rebel base the Empire is about to take over would be ideal for a yoga retreat. We dwell in the possible. Namaste.

The Pseudoscience That Will Enable Tom Brady to Play into His Nineties

Author's Note: This story was written and published during the 2019 season, Tom Brady's last with the New England Patriots. His subsequent signing with the Tampa Bay Buccaneers, along with his retirement/unretirement proves, once again, that truth is stranger than fiction.

Age 42: The rest of the 2019–2020 season. Keep doing the TB12 Method: Wake up each morning at 6 a.m. without an alarm. Drink 20 ounces of water infused with TB12 electrolytes. Breakfast is a smoothie consisting of bananas, blueberries, seeds, and nuts. 8 a.m. workout focusing on muscle pliability. Follow workout with protein shake made from TB12 protein powder. Lunch includes a salad with fish. Snacks range from nuts to berries to TB12 protein bars. Dinner of chicken and roasted alkalizing, anti-inflammatory vegetables like broccoli, carrots, cucumbers, green beans, sweet potatoes, and zucchini. Avoid: alcohol, sugar, processed foods, trans fats. After dinner spend 45 minutes studying the playbook in soft, diffuse light. Do not use nightshade vegetables like tomatoes, bell peppers, or eggplant in raw, uncooked lampshades. Relax by watching *Tom vs. Time* and brainstorm ideas for next season's *Tom vs. Downtime*. Drink 12 glasses of water a day. Do cognitive destress exercises before going to sleep in a cold, dark room. Lights out by 9 p.m.

Ages 43–45. Enhance the TB12 Method: Wake up each morning at 6 a.m. to the sound of mourning doves cooing. Drink 24 ounces of water infused with TB12 maximum diffusing electrolyte umbrella. Add TB12 baking soda tablets to breakfast smoothie to increase alkalizing, anti-inflammatory effects. Increase muscle elasticity with "extra stretchy" rubber band exercises. Have pizza "once in a while" to avoid the stress-related cortisol of pizza deprivation. Continue to follow TB12 diet for snacks, lunch, and dinner. Watch *Tom vs. Downtime* while brainstorming ideas for next season's *Tom vs. Grandfather Clocks*, a docuseries in which Tom travels the country fixing up old grandfather clocks found at antique shops. Drink 15 glasses of water a day. Do cognitive destress exercises before going to sleep in a colder, darker room. Go night-night by 8:45. Cryogenically freeze stem cells harvested from offspring.

Ages 45–48. Continue to follow and refine the TB12 Method. Wake up each morning at 6 a.m. to pseudoscientifically proven "Best Songs to Wake Up To," including Coldplay's "Viva La Vida," St. Lucia's "Elevate," Bill Withers' "Lovely Day" and Wham!'s "Wake Me Up Before You Go-Go." Slurp 26 ounces of water from cucumbers soaked in TB12 electrolyte solution. Drink a breakfast smoothie of chalk and blueberries. After the patented TB12 "Gumby" workout, eat a banana, including the peel. Watch *Tom vs. Grandfather Clocks* while brainstorming ideas for *Tom vs. B.C. Time*, a series of fitness videos filmed at locations significant on the B.C. timeline including Machu Picchu, Stonehenge, the Great Wall of China, and the Parthenon. Start a social media campaign to raise awareness of nightshade vegetables being used to manufacture lampshades for children. Drink 18 glasses of water per day. Go to sleep by 8:30 in a dark walk-in freezer. Spend off-seasons in private flotation chamber doing R.E.S.T. therapy (Really Easy Sleepy Time). Extend the Patriots shotgun formation to a long barrel shotgun formation. Start wearing a helmet on top of helmet. Unveil the latest brainchild of Josh Daniels and Bill Belichick: a "Wild Tom" offense with only running plays.

Age 49. Hire 6 Tibetan monks to chant each morning for a 6 a.m. wake-up. Absorb 26 ounces of electrolyte-infused water through TB12 osmosis chamber. Breakfast is a smoothie composed of antacids and toothpaste. After 8 a.m. TB12 "Mushy Muscle" workout, suck on alkaline batteries. Eat sensibly for lunch, dinner, and snacks. Get photographed eating chocolate and fast foods so people see the "human side" of TB. After photographs, spit out food and replenish saliva immediately. Watch *Tom vs. B.C. Time* while brainstorming ideas for *Tom vs. Geologic Time*, a docuseries in which Tom does high-velocity, force-dispersing exercises using fossils of geologic eras from the Cenozoic all the way through the Paleoproterozoic.
Surprise opponents by changing the main formation of the Wild Tom offense with a sawed-off shotgun formation followed by an Uzi formation in Super Bowl LXI. Lobby congress to create a new Patriot Act that does not apply to Patriots players so that massage parlors can forgo surveillance. Visit a massage parlor after every game.

Age 50. Auction off the opportunity to wake Tom up at 6 a.m. with a single snap of the fingers and then sit down and drink 28 ounces of TB12 electrolyte-infused water while sharing with TB the ways his career has been inspirational. Breakfast is a smoothie composed of plaster and lithium varnish. Follow 8 a.m. TB12 "Supple Baby Bottom" workout with a protein shake with potassium hydroxide extracted from printing inks. Lunch is fish stuffed with raisins. Dinner is raisins stuffed with fish. After practices and games, visit an acupuncturist to receive needle treatment for inflammation and infrared lamp treatment for detoxification. Incorporate AK-47 formation into Wild Tom offense, which includes a second QB so that Tom only hands off to other QB that then hands off to a defensive tackle converted to tailback.

Age 51. Retire from the QB position. Spend five years floating in the new TB12 chamber aboard the International Space Station to avoid the effects of gravity. Subsist by licking ceramic glazes for lithium, taking TB12 alkalizing pills made from luminescent varnish and pyrotechnics, and drinking 20 glasses of electrolyte-infused water per day.

Age 57. Return to Earth to enter the Pro Football Hall of Fame. Surprise the audience by cutting speech short with, "I got a game to play." Arrive at the Hall of Fame game and play one game for the Miami Dolphins, then fax their playbook to the New York Jets after doctoring it so that it appears misleading. Return to Patriots training camp after tweeting condescending "As if" photo of playing in a Dolphins uniform. Begin career as a holder for the son of Stephen Gostkowski.

Ages 58–78. In the off-season, undergo a surgical procedure to remove lungs and install gills and gill capillaries along the side of the neck. After surgery attach permanent TB12 Aquaman suit that doubles as a Patriots uniform and includes a water tank/flow system to continually pump water enhanced with electrolytes to TB gills. The suit includes fin fingers for the perfect field goal hold. Continue to follow the TB12 method. Wake up each morning to sunrise's gentle eyelid kiss. Pump 30 ounces of electrolyte-infused water through TB12 Aquaman suit. For 8 a.m. workout, swim 3 miles in a spa pool that uses a paddle wheel to generate an opposing current. Instead of meals and snacks, gnaw on dyed furs sprinkled with gunpowder periodically throughout the day. Occasionally have avocado ice cream topped with nuts as a treat. Go to sleep in a cold, dark fish tank by 8 p.m.

Ages 78–91. Travel to South America to undergo transfusion of blood from llamas and vicunas from the Andean mountains. Apply osteographs from pig cortical bones to increase overall bone density and decrease the likelihood of injury. Undergo a bone transplant of rhino femurs. Continue to follow the TB12 method.

Beyond Age 91. Pending pseudoscientific stem cell development, consider return to the QB position.

APPLE CORE UPSETS THE STATUS QUO

PINEAPPLE CROWN

I now call this meeting to order. Apple, the floor is yours.

APPLE CORE

Thank you. Eight score and four years ago, a member of our family, little known at the time, made the trip from the squalor of Panama to the greatest city in the world *(winks at PEAR CORE),* known as the Big Apple. Once arrived, due to the lack of trash cans, this fruit, like so many, was left to rot in the streets. The inverse relationship between decay and friction led to slipping in the streets, causing widespread broken limbs, some of which had to be amputated. It wasn't long before a vaudeville performer known as "Sliding" Billy Watson, desperate for fame, usurped this risk to public health in the name of physical comedy. From there it was a short toss to the silver screen, where silent film stars like Charlie Chaplin seized on this remorseless schadenfreude and called it slapstick. And the rest—a century of egregious monopoly on all exocarpic humorous appeal—is, as they say, history.

PEACH PIT

Speak plainly. What are you saying?

PEAR CORE

Maybe Apple would if you wouldn't interrupt.

APPLE CORE

That's fine, my goodly Pear. I can speak for myself. I'm referring, of course, to Banana Peel. But this is no history lesson. Rather, it's a call to action. Fruits, it is time to be funny. All of us can be symbols of comedy. Why should Banana Peel be the only one?

PEACH PIT

Come off it. You can't be serious. Banana peels are floppy, yellow, slippery. They're hilarious. Monkeys eat bananas. "Go bananas" is an expression. Did you grow underground? Have you no eyes? Tell me, what is humorous about my wrinkled outer core?

PLUM PIT

I know it all too well. We are a humorless bunch. At least you have 90210.

ORANGE PEEL

Peach is right. We could never compete with the floppy yellow tails, the history of falls. That noise on cartoons when someone slips.

MOLDY PUMPKIN

Grgryrlllyplbvvvdr.

WATERMELON RIND

It's true. The same fate as Moldy Pumpkin awaits us all. If not mold, then it's the compost bin. Do you not fear the worms, writhing in the darkness? What is funny about our decaying? Where is the humor in a slow demise?

(APPLE CORE hesitates.)

PEAR CORE

Tell them, Apple. Tell them about your plan. Just like you whispered to me, last night. It's magnificent. Tell them.

APPLE CORE

(Rolls toward center.) I believe that all of us have the potential to be funny in the face of such darkness. Banana Peel is not unique in having comedic properties. Rather it is a question of outlook, confidence. If each—

PEACH PIT
We are born this way. Better to accept our true identity
and seek suitable soil for our seeds.

APPLE CORE
To sleep, perchance to dream—aye, there's the rub.

ORANGE PEEL
I'll never be funny. How can I have appeal? No one even
peels me right! I always end up ripped to pieces.

GRAPE STEM
I'm thin and prickly.

LEMON WEDGE
How can I make puckered lips smile?

*(STRAWBERRY LEAVES bursts into tears. CHERRY
PIT rolls over to soothe.)*

WATERMELON RIND
It's hopeless. Life is hopeless. Bring on the worms.

MOLDY PUMPKIN
Grgryrlllyplbvvvdr.

APPLE CORE
My sweet ones, do you not hear yourselves? Do you
not have ears? Orange Peel, who says you have to be torn
into odd shapes? I tell you, if a floppy yellow peel can be
funny, then we can too. I am a mere core, chewed and
browning; what incentive do I have to lie? This is our
birthright. All fruit, everywhere, can be funny. *(He rolls
around, getting animated, gesturing forcefully.)* There is
something amusing about each and every one of us. Look

at Pear. Tell me that a pear-shaped body isn't an opportunity for self-deprecating humor?

PEAR CORE

It is my shape. I cannot change.

APPLE CORE

We are depriving ourselves of more than just giggles. I tell you, we are renouncing liberty itself! The freedom to inspire laughter at the end of our lives. This shouldn't be limited to bananas. All fruits are created equally funny.

(The hall erupts in a din of fierce arguing. PEACH PIT charges APPLE CORE. PEAR CORE faints. The rinds try to break up the melee.)

PINEAPPLE CROWN

Order! Order!

CANTALOUPE RIND

(Shouting) KNOCK IT OFF!

(Silence ensues. APPLE CORE and PEACH PIT are separated.)

CANTALOUPE RIND

Look at me. Pale. Buff. Ridges arranged in a mesh pattern. I look like an old net. All my life I've thought that about myself. That I'm just this pale net and someday I'll rot as becomes all fruit that is born of flower. Sure, my seeds may grow anew. And that's been enough for me. But I've listened to what our learned fruit is saying. And now, for the first time since I was just a little sprout, I'm thinking that there might be more for me. More than crude breast humor. The warm sound of real, genuine laughter. Who knows, maybe a belly laugh or two? If a banana peel can do it, well, why can't I?

ORANGE PEEL
(*Over the outbursts of other fruit*) I've always wanted to be pithy!

KIWI SKIN
Your Crown, a visitor has arrived.

PINEAPPLE CROWN
Allow the visitor to enter.

(*A soggy tomato rolls in.*)

SOGGY TOMATO
I have heard the winged words spoken in this hall, and I've come to speak truth.

GRAPE STEM
You're just a vegetable. Get out of here!

SOGGY TOMATO
Aye. I thought that of myself once, too. Before I knew myself. Before I knew the truth. But lo, I am a fruit like ye.

(*The hall is filled with gasps. STRAWBERRY LEAVES begins wailing. CHERRY PIT leans over and consoles.*)

GRAPE STEM
Liar! You're a rotten vegetable.

(*In a dramatic gesture, SOGGY TOMATO rolls past PINEAPPLE CROWN, slicing itself open, spurting a gooey puddle of seeds.*)

PEACH PIT
Look! Seeds! It's true.

WATERMELON RIND

If a tomato is a fruit what else is out there? We're all lost, lost, lost.

MOLDY PUMPKIN

Grgryrlllyplbvvvdr.

SOGGY TOMATO

My dear edible friends, let me not mince words. I, too, once dreamed of laughter in the sunset, the warmth of comedy in the winter of life. I also felt the jealousy, nay, rage, at the fortune of Banana Peel. I, too, thought I could cause humans to fall.

GRAPE STEM

I don't care if it's oozing seeds. I'm telling you it's a vegetable. It could have gotten those seeds anywhere . . .

SOGGY TOMATO

But heed these words: I became not a source of laughter and light in the world, but an object of derision! Of shame! They hurled me at the unfunny! And the same will happen to you!

(The hall erupts again into fierce arguing. LEMON and LIME WEDGES restrain GRAPE STEM from assaulting SOGGY TOMATO.)

APPLE CORE

(Calling vainly above the shouts) Fruits! Fruits! If we all focus on our own unique gifts . . .

(A WALNUT SHELL and a PEANUT SHELL walk in.)

WALNUT SHELL

(To KIWI SKIN) What's all the hubbub?

KIWI SKIN
A matter between fruits.

PEANUT SHELL
Step aside, hairball. If you think we're not getting involved, you're nuts.

"Hello, thank you for calling Adopt-A-Highway. How may I help you?"

"Hi. Is this the information line?"

"Yes, this is the number for Adopt-A-Highway information."

"OK, good. I really need some information."

"Are you interested in adopting a stretch of California highway?"

"You mean, like, adoption? Like a kid? Like I would be a parent? To a highway?"

"A portion of it, yes, sort of. Your oversight would be similar to that of a parent-child relationship in that you would be responsible for the well-being of a portion of the road. But you won't have to change any diapers, if that's what you're worried about."

"Diapers? We're still talking about the highway, right? Or is it like a two-for-one deal, the highway *and* a kid? Like the kid comes with the road?"

"No, sir. I was just joking. It's a pretty humorless job so I try to kid around when I get the chance."

"Oh."

"So, are you still interested in a stretch of highway? Most people start with a two-mile section."

"Two miles? I'm sorry, but I'm going to have to pass. Even though it's only concrete with some yellow paint, it still sounds like more responsibility than I'm capable of at the moment."

"I understand. Is there anything else I can do for you today?"

"Yes. I was sort of hoping for some information . . ."

"If you have access to the internet, I can direct you to the Caltrans website, which has all the need-to-know information regarding adopting a highway as well as updates to all California Department of Transportation programs. For example, the annual Fall Cleanup Day has been canceled due to COVID-19."

"No no no, that's not the information I need."

"The Adopt-A-Highway program began in 1989, one of the truly successful public-private partnerships of our time. More than 120,000 Californians have cleaned and enhanced over 15,000 miles of highway shoulders."

"No. Stop. Please, stop. I mean, that's great. The highways should be cleaned up and all, it's just . . . I'm in serious need of information. Like, generally speaking."

"General information. All right. Perhaps you could tell me a little bit about yourself. You see, truth be told I don't really get all that many calls, and the ones I do get don't have much in the way of conversation."

"I'm forty-six years old and very much alone. I had what you would call a mental breakdown when I was twenty-one. I was an economics major at a prestigious university, but it all felt wrong. So I left. Started walking. For Alaska. I never made it, though. Found a little abandoned shack in the Yukon and made it my home. Learned to hunt with a crossbow. I lived in that tiny cabin for twenty-five years. In that time I've made peace with myself. And with God. I decided to come back. See what's out here."

"Wow, that's, um, some story. I'm forty-three and still live with my parents. I feel alone too. Tell me more."

"I came out of the wilderness just a few days ago. Hitchhiked along the highway—that's when I saw your sign. It had this number and said to call for information."

". . ."

"Are you still there?"

"Yes. I'm here. Go on."

"So . . . yeah. I got picked up, eventually. It took a while. Nice guy. Loaned me some money for a couple nights at a motel. Ended up at this small local inn. The clerk is this young gal. Maybe twenty years old, if that. She's always on this device, which turned out to be her phone. I asked her about it. And she told me. She says everyone has them, these…smart…phones. I think she was having fun with me. That's another reason I called. I really just need someone to talk to. Someone I can trust."

"You can talk to me."

"I appreciate that. I really do. You mentioned the internet. So did the gal. I don't know what that is."

"The internet is this thing that people use to get information. I think Al Gore started it or something. Hold on, let me google it."

"There's another one. The clerk said that one, too. Google. Never heard of it."

"Google is a search engine people use to find stuff on the internet."

"An engine, like in a car? I don't understand. I'm so confused, it's like I want to explode."

"You poor thing."

"I made a list of all the things I've never heard of. Well, the clerk helped me with it. She was pretty incredulous. But again, not in a good way. I've never heard of any of the following: Google, Amazon, Facebook, Twitter, Instagram, Wikipedia, Uber, Netflix, YouTube, Airbnb, Tinder."

"There's so much for us to talk about."

"The clerk said she would've told me, but she had a headache from playing beer pong all night. What's beer pong?"

"You didn't come across it at college? I mean, before you dropped out."

"No. I was sort of a loner."

"Beer pong is a drinking game. You arrange cups of beer in a triangle on each end of a ping pong table. Hold on, I'm googling it . . . Looks like it got started in the '50s in college fraternities. Dartmouth College is believed to be the first. Says it started with the use of paddles. Interesting, I've only played it where you throw the ball with your hands."

"You've played beer pong?"

"Yes. I'm not very proud of my college years. That's something else we can talk about. I feel like I can tell you anything. I see by the caller ID that you're up near Fort Bragg. I'm actually not too far away. I know the area. I get off in an hour. Want to grab a Starbucks?"

"What's Starbucks?"

"Oh, it doesn't matter, you silly, silly man. Nothing matters as long as we're together."

"I don't even know your name."

"I'll tell you my name. I'll tell you everything. The whole world. It's all in my pocket. I just need you to do one thing for me first."

"What?"

"A brief survey about customer satisfaction. Please say yes."

"Yes."

"I knew I could count on you. No matter what happens, stay on the line."

Gentle, Be Gentle, Thine Mint

Recently I picked up a new antiseptic mouthwash, based on a recommendation from my dentist. The other night my wife glanced at the new bottle on our counter and made a comment about the flavor: Gentle Mint.

"Gentle, huh? Don't want your mint to be too rough?"

So here, inspired by my wife's snarkiness, are two hypothetical conversations.

Number One: A Hypothetical Text Exchange

HUSBAND: Hey, honey, are you at the store?
WIFE: Yes
HUSBAND: Can you pick up my mouthwash?
WIFE: Sure
HUSBAND: Remember, don't get the Rough
        Mint. It's way too rough for my
        delicate gums!
WIFE: Obvi
HUSBAND: And also not regular mint. Even
        though it's regular. It's still just a tad
        on the rough side, mint wise.
WIFE: Got it. Gentle Mint. I know. Chasing our
      1 year old
HUSBAND: But remember last time you got
        Gently Gentle Mint. It was actually
        a little too gentle for me. I like the
        mint to be gentle, but not so gentle
        that I can't feel the gentleness.
        Thanks. Luv u
WIFE: I might kill you

Number Two: Board Meeting of Hypothetical Antiseptic Mouthwash Company

CEO

It's decided, we'll push both the Regular and Mint flavors. Agreed?

(ALMOST) EVERYONE AT THE LONG TABLE

Agreed. *(Almost all heads nod.)*

CEO

All right. Well, let's have a great quarter. Unless there's anything else, I'll call this meeting to adjournment. *(He pauses.)* This meeting is aaaaaddj—

GUY IN 7th SEAT ON THE RIGHT

Actually, sir, I—I have something.

CEO

All right, spit it out. Oh, shit, a pun. Well, let's hear it.

GUY IN 7th SEAT ON THE RIGHT

See, sir, I was thinking about the mint flavor. And I love mint. Believe me. I chew mint gum. Mint chocolate chip is my favorite ice cream. I drink mint juleps—in moderation, of course. I even have a mint air freshener in my car.

CEO

What in tarnation are you babbling about, son?

GUY IN 7th SEAT ON THE RIGHT

Well, sir, recently I bought some mint toothpaste from our competitor, you know, just, uh *(coughs nervously)*, to see what we're up against. And the mint, well, see, sir, it was um . . .

                              CEO
We haven't got all day!

               GUY IN 7th SEAT ON THE RIGHT
Rough. The mint was rough. It was way too rough. I
had flashbacks of my brother, as a kid. See, he was a real
rough-houser. He always played too rough. Mom would
shout, "Barry, you're playing too rough!" But would he
stop? No. He just played rougher. I still have scars from the
titty twisters.

                              CEO
I'm sorry to hear that. My older brother was too rough
with me quite often.

               GUY IN 7th SEAT ON THE RIGHT
See what I mean? Well, our competitor's toothpaste, the
mint is like that: too rough. But our new mouthwash, it's
not. It's just right, like the distance from the Earth to the
Sun and Goldilocks's porridge. It's not too strong and not
too weak. It's perfect. The mintiness, I mean.

                              CEO
I'm glad that you feel that way. And thank you for
speaking out.

               GUY IN 7th SEAT ON THE RIGHT
Yes, well, sir, I was thinking . . .

                              CEO
Yes, I'm listening.

               GUY IN 7th SEAT ON THE RIGHT
What if we added the word "Gentle" to the bottle?
Consumers would know that the mint is not too strong.

CEO

Genius! What did you say your name was? Doesn't matter, you're getting a promotion.

We haven't received any mail for three consecutive days, I tell my wife. Huh, she responds, on that line between statement and question. She is on Instagram. Something amusing, making her smile. She wants to keep watching. I think someone is taking our mail, I say. Monday, Tuesday, Wednesday. No mail? Not a single article? That's not right. Something is wrong. What? my wife says, stepping firmly into question territory. Something is wrong. Someone is taking our mail. She looks at me like I'm crazy. Why would anyone take our mail? I don't know, I say. I don't know. Well, she says, there's nothing we can do about it tonight. She is back on her phone. She is smiling again at whatever is on Instagram, a woman talking in a hot tub with a southern accent, wearing a visor.

Who wants to go get the mail with Daddy? No one does. Not anymore. It used to be a highlight of the day. Getting the mail with Daddy. That was at the beginning of the pandemic. We pretended to ride horses, airplanes, spaceships . . . For months we were unicorns, soaring . . . We rode scooters, bikes . . . I was pulling them on wagons. It was a good break, getting outdoors, a burst of exercise in the twilight.

Sometimes there was a fight over who got to use the key, who got to carry what. A pink envelope? Forget about it. American Girl doll catalog? Goodnight Irene . . . Does anyone want to go get the mail? But they are all on screens, tired from a long day of being on screens. All right, well, I'm going to get the mail. I walk down by myself in the late afternoon to the mailbox. There is nothing. I see Ted, pulling his garbage to the curb. Are you getting your mail? I ask Ted. He acts like I'm asking him if he's doing makeup experiments on monkeys in his basement. Maybe he is confused, like maybe I'm asking if he's getting it, physically, himself, right now. I haven't been getting my mail this week, I say. Oh, he says. We're getting ours. Not like there's ever anything good! I laugh that laugh you make when you pretend something is minimally funny, has crossed the Threshold of Least. Ted gives a shrug that says, sometimes these things happen, and goes back to get his recycling bin. I stand by the mailbox and think for a minute, watching the clouds march west. I can see it will be a beautiful sunset, once the sun gets low enough. My mailbox is empty.

The mail is held together in two big, thick stacks.

It is late afternoon. I've come back empty-handed again, so I sit down on the curb to think. Maybe it is the postal worker? He seems a rather careless fellow. There was that time I came around the corner and he ran a stop sign and almost T-boned me. I remember it was a Sunday, and it was strange to see him. I shook my head at him, and since then have heard several tales corroborating that his driving is reckless. I told this to John one day and he shared some incidents where the postal worker drove by and *threw* packages out the window. John used the expression "homeboy." Homeboy straight up tossed a box out the window, he said.

The postal worker comes in the mornings, but I don't know what time. Amanda comes by walking her pug, Wiley. She lives right across from the mailbox. I decide to ask her if she knows when the postal worker comes. Huh? she says, as if I'm insulting Wiley's little striped socks. I ask again. I don't know, she says, I think around 10:30. Why? she asks. I tell her. She raises her eyebrows, nodding, and says huh again. She looks down at Wiley, as if he might comment also, but he only pants with his tongue out. That's strange, she says. It is, isn't it? I say. It'll probably come tomorrow, she says, and they walk on. Wiley's little socked feet make scratching sounds on the sidewalk. I am always working at 10:30.

Do you think the postal worker is taking our mail? I ask my wife that night in bed. Why would he do that? she asks. I don't know, I don't know. She is on Facebook. Why don't you call the post office tomorrow if you are that worried about it? I think I will. Is there anything you are waiting for in the mail? Not especially. All our packages come to the door. I know. So what are you worried about? It's just strange. Why wouldn't we get any mail at all? Four days now. Just call them.

Each stack has a thick rubber band around it.

My neighbor Bill works for the post office. He is high up. He works from home now, too, during the pandemic. We used to come home at the same time, shoot the bull in our driveways, joke about how one person won if they pulled in twenty seconds earlier. I haven't seen Bill in months. My wife says Bill's mom had a stroke. I wish I could ask Bill, I think, as I sit on hold. I'm on hold a long time. I have to get back to work. I hang up.

The first stack is full of catalogs, magazines, and coupon mailers.

On Friday I walk to get the mail and a neighborhood kid is sitting on top of the mailboxes. He's a sneaky kid, always casting furtive glances, like he's up to something. I forget his name. Starts with an *s*. He was in Daisy's class a few years ago, in first grade. When I volunteered in the class, he called me "dude."

Once Daisy was sitting on the mailboxes and Bill walked up. I wouldn't sit on that, Daisy, Bill said. He said it in a nice way, with a smile. He's a nice guy. One time, halfway through the pandemic, he told me how highly accurate the mail system is, how rare it is for them to lose even one letter. He spoke extensively about his confidence in the system to handle mail-in ballots during the election. Bill is a good guy. I hope his mom is OK. It's extremely rare for

them to lose even one letter, he said. He used the word
"extremely." When they lose a letter, it is usually the fault
of the carrier, he said. But that is one letter, let alone a
week's worth of mail. He said the percentage of loss is less
than a tenth of a percent.

The kid jumps off the mailbox and takes off on his
scooter. He shoots one of his glances back at me. Sawyer.
That's his name. Like Tom Sawyer. Maybe he is stealing our
mail.

*The second stack is a pile of envelopes, most of which are bills or
junk.*

On Monday there is a crowd of people by the mailbox.
I knew something was up. There are a bunch of kids and
two adults: Lyla and Julie. I see that they both have an
armful of mail. They are always on top of anything
happening in our neighborhood. If something is going
down, like someone is going to move, they are always the
first to know about it. As I get closer, I see and hear what
the issue is. There's a Missing Cat sign. A brown tabby
named Rusty. Friendly, not likely to leave the
neighborhood, the sign says. I am standing on the fringe of
the crowd. Some of the kids have seen the cat. Some of
them know Rusty, or Rusters, as they call him. A search
party is formed. There is a sense of urgency. The kids are
shouting facts about the case. The cat has been missing for
24 hours! Last seen on So-and-So's fence! One group is
dispatched to make Find Rusters signs. The kids all rush
off in groups to search different areas. They keep shouting.
Not likely to leave the neighborhood! Lyla and Julie smile
at me. The smiles are because the kids are so excited, so
serious. Julie's daughter is clamoring to go home and get a
magnifying glass, to look for clues. Julie responds with that
lilting voice adults use with kids when the subject matter is
absurd. There might be whiskers, her daughter says. Mark
comes up and gets his mail. All those kids are going to find

are bones, he says. Coyotes. That cat doesn't have a chance. Everyone leaves. I check my mailbox and it is empty. I look over and Sawyer is watching me.

The junk mail consists of flyers for credit cards, car insurance, and a new cable subscription, plus an envelope that says URGENT: REFINANCE NOW! SAVE BIG $.

I have left two messages and sent an email, neither of which have received a reply from the post office. This is very troubling. I ask my wife: Do you think I should call Bill? What's he going to do? I don't know, I say. She is watching an episode of a show about long-lost families. He might be able to look into it, I say. Leave him alone, she says. His mom is sick. She had a stroke. Are you expecting anything? No. Not that I can think of. Why do you care so much? I don't know. It's just strange.

There is a blue envelope at the bottom of the second stack. It is a letter from my uncle wishing me a Happy Easter.

I can't sleep. I'm lying next to my wife, listening to her breathing, when I remember. I am expecting something important: my new ATM card. I haven't used cash since the pandemic began. My ATM card has expired. What do you need cash for? she says the next morning. I am tired and irritable. I spill coffee on my shirt. I don't know. I might need it, I say, wiping at the stain.

I am walking down the street, empty-handed, back from the mailbox. The Missing Cat sign is still there. The sun is setting and I am moving from sunlight to shade in the patterns of all the trees that are planted equidistant from each other. Ted calls them parking lot trees. They are rather plain, waving in the breeze, which is coming from the west, the ocean. Amanda walks by. Today Wiley's socks are bright yellow.

The kids down the street are playing baseball. The street runs downhill at about an eight percent grade, I'd say, and every time the ball gets past the catcher they have to chase after it. I hear a sound like a rock landing in the bushes to my right. Did someone just throw a rock at me?

I look over to my left and Sawyer is standing there. He takes off on his scooter.

There is a bundle of magazines at the bottom of one stack. An alumni magazine. An education magazine from a teacher's union. Writer's Digest. Good Housekeeping. People. There are many catalogs for the clothing companies that my wife buys clothes from. There is one clothing company that sends me catalogs, because of a shirt I got for my birthday that was too big. I had to return the shirt for another size and they got my address. The clothes are über-expensive. $40 for a T-shirt, faded to look retro. Now they send me catalogs every month. I think I should try to get off their list, but it's doubtful that I will actually take the time to do this.

I call the bank to cancel the ATM card. They don't have a record of my request for a new card. I send another email, leave another message for the post office. Rusters still hasn't been found. The kids form nightly search brigades. The adults think it's cute how the kids are all working together. A paw print is found on a nearby trail. Sawyer glares at me when he rides by on his scooter. I manage to get outside at 10:30 for our delivery and the postal worker is just leaving our mailbox. He is driving fast, too fast for a residential street. I wave for him to stop, or at least slow down, but he acts like he doesn't see me, like I'm invisible, like I'm not standing on the curb waving my arms, saying hey, excuse me, sir, sir.

There are envelopes requesting donations from charities that have received them in the past. Doctors Without Borders. The zoo. The children's museum. The food bank. The homeless shelter. Things are dire, because of the pandemic.

I write a note and put it in our box.

I put our address, even though it's redundant. The next two days, every time I hear the doorbell, I think it is him, but he doesn't stop by.

There is a small envelope for my wife from Brittany, likely a Thank You note for throwing a baby shower. Brittany is pregnant with her second child.

When it's for a second baby, it's called a sprinkle instead of a shower, my wife says when she is ordering the cake one night in bed.

Do you know that it has been almost two weeks since we've received any mail, I am about to say, but I know she is busy picking out frosting. That's when I remember that I also ordered checks. The checks and the ATM card. Also, tax season is coming. I am very concerned.

I am outside at ten. I am missing work for an illness that I do not really have. I am walking in circles, pretending that I am on a walk but really staking out the mailbox. The driver doesn't come. Did I miss him? Did he come earlier? Has the delivery time changed? No one is around. It's the middle of the morning on a weekday. People are working, making a difference. This can't go on. The only person I see for the entire hour is a plumber. He stops at Ted's. Something is wrong. Something is definitely very wrong. Why won't they call me back or respond to my emails or my note? I keep leaving more and more messages, each time less formal and less polite. There must be an explanation. Things like this don't happen without an explanation.

Later I am sitting on the curb and Amanda and Wiley walk by. I ask about the socks. Wiley has arthritis, she says. They provide traction, keep him from splaying.

There is a bill from the HOA. I have been meaning to go paperless but it's just one of those things, like the catalog for the expensive clothes, except that I think one day I will eventually go paperless.

Why do I care so much? My wife doesn't care. It is true that the mail is mostly junk. Another week goes by and I slowly, with great effort and deep breathing exercises, decide that I don't care either. It's just mail. It will work itself out. With the pandemic and everything, there is so much happening in the world that does matter and is important, and one person not getting their mail is hardly pressing. My fretting is disparate to the problem. It has no effect on The Big Picture. It's small potatoes. So what if the postal worker (or Sawyer!) is messing with the mail. The ATM card and the checks are not more important than my mental health. I start laughing. It's funny. I had been worried *sick* about something so trivial. I ask my wife, Can you imagine Sawyer trying to cash a check for a million dollars? What are you talking about? Nothing I say, and kiss her hard, on the mouth.

The tension of each rubber band is proportionate to the mass of the bundle.

I am waking up in the morning now and going for jogs. Each day I run farther. I am up to five miles. When I come back, sweating and out of breath, I coast past the mailbox and it seems like a symbol of everything I used to value that really has no value. When I see people getting mail, carrying their armfuls of envelopes and catalogs and boxes, or I see them getting the extra key which means they should open another mailbox to receive a package, the key left dangling in the package box door that is always left slightly ajar, I realize that these people are going day after day, week after week, month after month, year after year, every day except Sunday, for something that is essentially meaningless. This is a meaningless task, I say to myself. There is nothing that they are getting out of this, nothing important. It is all trivial and outdated. Catalogs for overpriced, superfluous goods. Everything important can be done online. Emails. Autopay. It won't be long until the mail is completely obsolete. I am ahead of the curve, therefore, in not performing this ritual.

The address on the Easter card, though legible, is not level. The downhill grade of the address is approximately the same as the grade of our street.

My daughter asks, Do you want to go get the mail, Daddy? I pick her up and twirl her in the air. I swoop her down between my legs. I tickle her. She is giggling and then laughing so hard it hurts. She runs, but I grab her and twirl her in the air again. I look deep into her eyes and store away this memory for when I am old and infirm and she is out living her life.

I would get the mail with you if it was on Neptune, I say. Where's Neptwo? she says. I twirl her in the air again and again, then swoop her down and feel the laughter shaking her ribs.

I wake up in a panic. Tax season is getting closer. I haven't received my W-2. I try to send an email to HR, but I'm so anxious my fingers won't cooperate. I try to log in to my checking account, but I keep receiving the same message: Invalid Password. Is someone using my checks, after all? Would Sawyer, a third grader, be sophisticated enough to change my password? I check my spam folder. Why haven't I received any response from any of my inquiries? I call Bill. It's the middle of the night. I leave a message, my voice frantic.

In the morning I wake up and run farther than I've ever run before. Seven miles. I feel calm when I return, walking past the mailbox, feeling my pulse.

And that is how it goes for another week. I am calm during the day but wake up in a panic. I call Bill, but his voicemail is full. I need answers. I cannot accept that something like missing mail has no explanation, is in fact random and without cause. There must be an explanation. In the mornings I run farther and farther, my lungs screaming for air, my legs burning, until the calm comes. I am doing better than ever at work. You've been doing a great job lately, Daddy, my wife says in front of the kids. I like this you, she says. This happier you. Let's keep him around, she says. When the kids aren't looking, she pinches my bottom.

But I know something has to give. I also know that Sawyer's mom makes him go out for a 1:30. I miss work for another day. I climb the hill with binoculars and watch him ride and stop at the mailbox. He is doing something. I am running down the hill. This is my chance to catch him in the act. I am running fast down the hill, faster than I have in years. I feel my foot catch a rock. My body is going forward but my foot, for a moment, isn't. I am falling. I am tumbling. I am in bushes getting scraped and cut. I hit something solid and everything goes dark.

I am home from a day in the hospital. They kept me overnight, for observation. There is a bandage on my forehead. The doorbell rings. It is the postal worker. He is wearing a loose mask that doesn't cover his nose. I see this from the couch. He hands each of my daughters a big bundle of mail. They bring the bundles inside. Hand them to me, I say. They want to start digging through them. In fact, my oldest does begin rifling through the first stack. Hand them to me now, I say in the quiet voice they know means business. They hand them to me, reluctantly. The top stack contains a note. I don't remember putting our mail on hold, I tell my wife. There must be some explanation, she says.

Join the MusiQ Revolution Today

From the forefront of music, technology, health, and the environment comes a new music streaming service destined to revolutionize the individual listening experience: MusiQ.

Ready for download on your smartphone or compatible device, MusiQ is designed to maximize the psychological, sociological, and environmental experience of listening to music.

With the arrival of MusiQ, current streaming services from companies like Spotify, Google, Amazon, and Apple are instantly outdated and obsolete. These antiquated services offer millions of songs with inaccurate claims like "unlimited." However, MusiQ offers the first truly unlimited musical experience. With quadrillions of songs, MusiQ includes the entire range of anything anywhere remotely close to being considered music. Every song ever made from every genre and culture since humans began recording music? You bet. How about acoustical engineering tracks like 10,000-year-old chanting from French caves made from synthetic echoes? Please. Musical speed bumps on a road in Japan? Don't make us laugh. MusiQ has exponentially more music than any person could ever listen to in a single lifetime, but that's just the start of what makes MusiQ the streaming service to end all streaming services.

MusiQ is designed with unique software that goes beyond simple learning and *masters* the musical tastes and preferences of every individual that downloads our service (a number growing every day). And that's not even the best part. MusiQ is free. From the very first note.

That's right. No sneaky two-month trial that leads to exorbitant charges. Sign a data sharing agreement and the door opens to a vast world of musical enjoyment right at your fingertips.

And sure, you could use your fingertips. Or your voice. You could tell the Q to play your favorite song. But this is where the design of MusiQ blasts off into a whole new stratosphere. Other services build playlists and recommendations based on songs you play. MusiQ does that (in its sleep), but right after downloading, by taking the simple step of connecting your email and social media accounts to the MusiQloud, your Q becomes connected with your life and experiences. Q will begin to anticipate songs you need to hear at any given moment.

And that's the first day. By enabling location on your smartphone, your Q will base music recommendations on local weather, traffic, and even your movement. Need a sunny song on a rainy day? Q is on it. Stuck in a traffic jam or hitting the open road? Q will know just the right driving tune. From your morning jog to washing the dinner dishes at the same time every night, Q will learn your routines and know just what to play.

Incredible as it seems, this is only the beginning of how MusiQ gets to know you and meets your musical needs. After a week of listening, a drone will deliver your Qpatch: a paper-thin adhesive matched to your skin color no larger than your thumbnail. When you agree to our terms with a thumbprint and selfie, we'll be able to guarantee that your Qpatch is an exact match. And this is where MusiQ blows the competition away with its technological, health-enhancing, and environmental prowess.

By adhering the undetectable, waterproof, and comfortable Qpatch to your temple, MusiQ will use its brainwave-sensing technology to learn even more about you and the type of music you like to listen to. Now in addition to GPS location and satellite weather reports, MusiQ will begin to home in on your unique moods, feelings, emotions, and even memories. It will detect and synthesize activity in the amygdala, the hippocampus, the cerebellum, and the prefrontal cortex, so that by the time your patch disintegrates, MusiQ will know you down to your most intimate fears and desires. And once we're there, playing music is child's play.

Amazed by the power and reach of our design? We're only getting started. After two weeks of use, MusiQ algorithms will analyze the songs from your library to distill your selections to their musical essence. Now you won't have to spend three minutes to gain the emotional benefit to either your sympathetic or parasympathetic nervous system. Need to get psyched for a workout? Give it two seconds. Want to experience a three-hour concert, but don't have the time? Consider yourself in the front row. And especially when you're feeling stressed out and tense, a S.O.N.G. is already in the Q.

MusiQ's S.O.N.G.S. technology (Sonar Omnirange Nano GigS) instantly delivers musical satisfaction to your brain. With this stroke of technological advancement, MusiQ is able to save and stockpile the most precious of human resources: time. Extra time to dedicate to your own well-being—emotional, physical, and mental.

But what about the environment? We thought you'd never ask. After one month of using MusiQ's streaming service, with your health and well-being at an all-time high, S.O.N.G.S. will begin to guide you to our closest Green Zone. Sounds harnessing your deepest desires and fears will lead you to a place designed for one specific purpose: to save the Earth.

By subscribing to MusiQ, you'll not only be getting the most technologically advanced music streaming service tailored to the very cells in the depths of your brain, you'll also be SAVING THE PLANET. What better way to spend those precious minutes that MusiQ has conserved than by helping develop geothermal energy solutions to the dire existential threat facing all of us?

The choice is yours. And it is a choice. Sure, you could be selfish and drive around a gas-guzzling SUV, listening to random music on another streaming service created by some bloated tech company that rakes in billions every year and treats our planet like its personal trash can. Or you could join MusiQ and do something for your grandchildren's grandchildren (while listening to your own *get 'er done* playlist, of course).

Riverview Terrace Pool and Spa Rules

Riverview Terrace Neighborhood Swim Center
Pool & Spa Hours: Sunday thru Thursday
11:00 a.m. until 7:00 p.m.
Friday and Saturday 8:00 a.m. until 8:00 p.m.
Note: Each day the pool will be closed at 4:20 for "a
little while." Like ten minutes or so.

1. Association facilities are reserved for full-time residents of the Association and their guests. Owners who have rented or leased their properties turn their rights over to the tenants. We know you will probably still show up and use the hot tub, but just don't be obvious about it. We also know that many residents will use the term "guests" very liberally. Again, just don't flaunt it. I really hate that.

2. No glass or sharp objects are allowed in the pool or spa. If there is broken glass in the pool area, the pool must be shut down until the pool is cleaned and the area is vacuumed. It's a major hassle. The last time it happened, it was a bottle of Miller High Life. You'd think a ritzy neighborhood like Riverview Terrace would be drinking imported beers like Heineken, but no. Last Memorial Day this dude in a visor (probably a guest—see Rule #1) is guzzling the "champagne of beers" and drops number nine of his twelve pack. Wasn't even using a koozie or trying to hide it. Slipped right through his fingers. Talk about your party foul. So no, Mr. Lifeguard Man won't "chill" when your guest, loud-ass red-visor dude, shatters his shitty beer. The residents responsible will be charged the pool cleaning fee.

3. The American Medical Association strongly recommends that children under the age of 5 are not exposed to the high temperature of the spa (104 degrees). The Association strongly urges parents to adhere to this warning, which we know you'll ignore no matter who

recommends it or how "strongly" they urge. I could drop some EXTRA STRENGTH recommendations on you right here, urge out the wazoo, but you and I both know that if the Good Lord Him or Her or Itself came down and frowned on it, you would still let your 3-year-old in. Nice job, American Medical Association. Keep on recommending stuff.

4. Children in diapers must wear rubber pants or swim diapers while in the pool. **(Children who do not have rubber pants with swim diapers are not permitted in the pool. THAT INCLUDES DISPOSABLE SWIM DIAPERS).** See what I did there? I went from **bold** to **ALL CAPS BOLD** to let you know that, unlike the AMA, I mean business. I don't care if I have to check for myself and risk getting labeled a sex offender—your kid isn't getting into the pool without **RUBBER**. Like skintight. I don't care where you get it. Get it, or don't bother showing up. I won't even go into the incident last August with brown splats dripping right along with footprints running to the women's room. I won't go into it except to say that I think I proved I'll come into the women's bathroom if I have to. Just get a rubber diaper, okay?

5. No weird oils. I can't.

6. Diving is not permitted. There's only 900 signs. If you dive in and smash your skull, I'm not saying you deserve it, but, seriously, I'm not even exaggerating about the signs. Much. There are a lot of signs, the upside-down frowny face with the red X. You seriously can't not see them.

7. Another one on guests. I could have put it as Rule #2, but I figured I would squeeze it in here down at #7 so you would think, He must be serious if he's coming back to it. Five guests per residence. Five. Not six. Not ten. Not five guests per resident. Five total. Cinco. Count with your fingers and only use one hand. And they must be **ACCOMPANIED** by a resident. See that? I just went bold and caps on your ass, right in the middle of the sentence,

with no lead-in. My chair is right by the gate. You think I'm going to let in your cousin that doesn't look anything like you? Not a chance. And FYI: Ever since red-visor dude, I carry a taser.

8. Lane-marker ropes and buoys are to be used exclusively for dividing swimming lanes. You'd be surprised.

9. No running, pushing, or boisterous activity in or around the pool or spa areas. (This includes kids on shoulders "chicken-fighting," throwing kids, pushing people into the pool, and football games. No warnings, especially you moms that say "don't run" but then go right back to reading your magazine. I can't stand that. Oh, and you might think it's funny when the Pool Guy gets hit by the football. You can laugh about it in the parking lot, wrestling your little Mahomes into a car seat.)

10. No smoking. And don't give me this "you saw smoke coming from the pool house during the 4:20 intermission" stuff. It's the pool house, and besides, what I do in there is my business.

11. Each resident is responsible for putting his/her/your 19 guests' litter in the trash receptacles prior to leaving. I'm not the Pool Maid. I'll let that shit pile up and we'll have ants and bees and rats and everything else. I will. And when some other neighbor's kid gets stung the day after you leave your Coors Lite cans (seriously what is it with rich people drinking shitty beer?) and little thin trendy alcoholic seltzer cans and sandwich wrappers and chip bags and pizza crusts and nasty-ass ranch plastic ramekins, I'll act like it didn't even happen, like I'm far away on some island drinking out of a coconut. That's *exactly* what I'll do.

12. No large floating devices. As a rule of thumb, anything larger than this sign is prohibited. And it's a big sign, right? Yeah, I know it is. It's a big-ass sign, so don't bring in that giant pink flamingo floaty that will piss everyone off. I guess you can still bring in noodles, because

someone complained to my boss and made this whole stink, but whatever. You get boisterous with that thing and it's mine. Got a nice little collection. Thinking about going into the pool noodle business, actually. Don't think I won't rip that shit right out of your kids' spoiled hands.

13. No loud music. Seriously, I know you can afford those fancy earbuds.

14. Leave me alone. I'm a pool guy. I have enough friends.

The tournament on the fourth day was much better. Kitty sat between Orenthal and me along the ropes near the green, and Gordon and Whitaker went up above to the tents. Shelton was the whole show. I do not think Kitty saw any other golfer. No one else did either, except the reporters who had to. It was all Shelton.

He was playing with two other golfers but they did not count. I sat beside Kitty and explained to her what it was all about. I told her about watching the cleek, not the ball, when the blade comes through swift and even. I got her to watch the golfer line up the blade of his cleek so that she saw what it was all about, so that it became something with a definite end rather than just a spectacle with unexplained knicker lengths and patterned socks. I had her watch how Shelton's caddy took the red flag away from the hole and held it so that it did not flap in the breeze, and how he showed Shelton, smoothly and suavely, the line of the break. She saw how Shelton avoided brusque movements with his jigger and saved the holes for when he wanted them, not whirly around the rim of the cup, but smoothly, into the center. She saw how Shelton worked the ball near the hole, and I pointed out to her the tricks other golfers used to make it look as though their ball was also near. She saw why she liked Shelton's jigger work and why she didn't like the others'.

Shelton never made any contortions; always it was straight and pure and natural in line. The others twisted themselves like corkscrews, their elbows raised, and leaned against the shafts of their cleeks after the ball ran past the hole to give a faked impression of the dangers of three-putting. Afterward, all that was faked turned bad and gave an unpleasant feeling. Shelton's putting gave real emotion, because he kept the absolute purity of the line in his movements and putts and always quietly and calmly took the ball from the bottom of the cup. He did not have to emphasize with his fist that his ball had gone into the hole. Kitty saw that something beautiful done close to the hole would be ridiculous if it were done a little way off. I told her how, since Hagen and Jones, all the golfers had been developing a technique that simulated the appearance of bogey danger in order to give a fake emotional feeling, while the par was really safe. Shelton had the old thing, the holding of his purity of line through the maximum exposure to the danger of bogey, while he dominated his competitors by making them realize that his score was unattainable, always accepting his cleek like an assassin preparing for killing.

"I've never seen him do an awkward swing," Kitty said.

"You won't until he gets frightened of three-putting," I said.

"He'll never be frightened," Orenthal said. "He's too damned good with his mashies and niblicks."

"He knew everything when he started. The others can't learn what he was born with."

"And God, what looks," Kitty said.

On the edge of the green, Shelton drew his jigger, rose on his toes, and sighted along the blade. The wind gusted as Shelton drew the blade back. Shelton's left hand dropped the face of the club over the ball, his left shoulder went forward as the blade moved, and, for just an instant, he and the ball were one. Shelton went out over the ball, the right arm extended high up to where the hilt of the jigger had gone, high on the hill's shoulder. Then the figure was broken. There was a little divot as Shelton came clear. Then he was standing, one hand up, facing the crowd, his red tie slipping out from under his jacket, blowing in the wind. The ball flying, the red tie, his other hand holding the jigger high like a sword, the ball coming to rest by the hole. Then the tie was gone, he was waving, his legs settling.

"There he goes," Orenthal said.

Shelton was close enough so the hole, if it had eyes, could see him. His cleek up, he whispered to the ball. He tapped one foot. Then he sighted along the blade of the cleek, his feet firm. He gathered himself in the wind. His caddy held the red flag tight. Then Shelton, standing close over the ball, his head forward, lifted the cleek slowly, the blade held low, then swung straight through, suddenly, two feet in the air. The ball disappeared and it was over.

Handkerchiefs were waving all along the green. The gallery did not want it ever to be finished. The club president looked down from his box and waved his handkerchief.

Shelton putted, not as he had been forced to, but as he wanted to. Boys were running toward him from all parts of the green, making a little circle around him. Others started to dance around the hole. The president whistled, and Shelton, running to get ahead of the crowd, grabbed one of the other golfers and cut off his ear. He leaned against the rope and gave Kitty the ear. He nodded and smiled. The crowd was all about him. The caddy released and replaced the red flag.

"You liked it?" Shelton called.

Kitty did not say anything. They looked at each other and smiled. Kitty held the ear in her hand.

"Don't get bloody," Shelton said, and then he grinned. The gallery wanted him. Several golfers shouted at Kitty. Shelton turned and tried to get through the crowd. They were all around him trying to lift him and put him on their shoulders. He fought and twisted away. He did not want to be carried on people's shoulders. But they held him and lifted him. It was uncomfortable and his legs were spraddled and his body was very sore. They were lifting him and all running toward the clubhouse. He had his hand on somebody's shoulder. He looked around at us apologetically. The crowd, running, left the course with him.

We all went back to the hotel. Kitty went upstairs. Orenthal and Gordon joined a large table. Whitaker and I sat and drank iced tea with lemonade at the bar. The iced tea and lemonade made everything seem better. I drank it without sugar and it was pleasantly bitter.

After a while Whitaker said, "Well, it was a swell tournament."

"Yes," I said. "It's like a wonderful nightmare."

"What's the matter? Feel low?"

"Low as hell."

"Have another iced tea and lemonade. Drink it slow."

It was beginning to get dark. The two of us sat at the bar and it seemed as though six people were missing.

"All right, everyone has their screen, their chocolate milk, their doughnut, their lollipop, and their stuffy. Good? Good. Now Daddy has a Zoom meeting with his agent, so no coming in the den. Okay? Okay."

I walked into the den, closed the door, sat down, and clicked Join.

The meeting host will let you in soon . . .

I noticed a booger on my shirt as the camera popped on. I flicked it off and ran a quick finger comb through my hair.

"Hi, Rebecca," I said.

"Hi, Sam."

"Good to talk with you today."

"Good to talk with you. I have news."

"Oh? Good news I hope?"

"I wouldn't say it's good, exactly," she said with a smile. "I'd say it's more like really, really, really good. Check that. I have great news."

"I'm all ears."

"The publishers have approved the final revisions and set a pub date. We're set to go."

I couldn't believe it. "I'm speechless," I mustered. We smiled at each other, and then I found the words. "I'm glad they came around. I thought we'd be going back and forth for months. Especially after all that haggling over glow balls. And I'm sorry, but I felt strongly that the word fangs doesn't belong anywhere near my story."

"Well, looks like they've acquiesced to everything on your list. Even the part about tucking in capes. I thought that was a long shot, but it worked. So did the eyeballs in the ball washers. They've kept it all."

"I'm so relieved. You don't know how much sleep I've been losing over those eyeball ball washers. I know there are no ball washers in a pandemic, but still. It sets up so much of the plot. When's the pub date?"

"They're targeting November 13, for a number of reasons. It happens to be a Friday the 13th, which goes with your greenskeeper werewolf. There are several vampire tie-ins which I will forward to you: anniversaries of various mob riots in famous cemeteries, vampire DNA extractions, vampire comic book release dates, and other significant paranormal activities sure to resonate. And finally, of course, it's the delayed Masters tournament."

"Okay. Wow. It's all happening so fast. I was expecting next year at the earliest. I'm always reading about how publishing moves at a glacial pace."

"Well, the glaciers are melting faster and faster, so I guess publishing has to keep pace!"

"Hahaha. Good one."

"No, seriously, they really think you've got something with your epic Vampire Golf Saga. How did they put it? Let me check my notes . . . Here it is. Quote, 'the nexus of golf fiction and YA vampire romance, with just the right mix of absurdist historical magical realism.' They really believe in you . . . so much that I've got one more surprise for you."

"I'm listening. Actually—can you give me one second?" I clicked the video off, muted myself, and poked my head out the door. "Who's screaming? Stop screaming. May, get everyone a squeezy Choco bar. Everyone gets a Choco bar. Yeeeeaaah! But only if we stop screaming."

I went back in and turned everything back on. "Sorry about that, you were saying, the last surprise?"

"They want to offer you a five-book deal for a full series, plus a sixth book, an offshoot of your genderless vampire caddy, Gory. They think there's a book there, maybe two."

"Wow. I'm pinching myself. This feels like a dream."

"There's only one teensy thing we need to talk about."

"I mean, I never stopped believing in myself. All these years. All the rejections. I've been saving them. Over two hundred. Factor in the ignored queries and it's over a thousand. The agent that laughed at me and said that vampire golf is the most ridiculous idea they've ever heard. I can still hear her laughter, see her face. A mole on the right cheek. In fact, the beer girl in chapter twelve, the real bitch—"

"Sam. The thing we need to talk about."

"Or the editor who wanted to make it vampire hockey. But no. I stuck to my guns. I didn't give up."

"Sam?"

"Yes."

"I understand you've got a lot of strong emotions right now. Believe me, I have them too. I've been rooting for you ever since you first queried me, all those years ago. I still remember the first line, 'What happens when a Count can't count his putts?' That's why we need to really focus on this last little detail."

"Okay. I'm listening. What is it?"

"Your name."

"My name?"

"Yes. The publishers want you to adopt a pen name. They think it will improve sales. You know, Sam Smith is such a common name. The singer, for one. I know you mentioned you wanted to release a Vampire Golf songbook, down the road. I think if you're serious about that project then we need to think seriously about a pen name."

"Well, you know, the thought has crossed my mind. I actually have a short list here. Can I read them and you give me your first impressions?"

"All right, shoot."

"The first is SammieE."

"SammieE?"

"Yeah." I spelled it for her. "I was thinking, you know, the ring of just one word, change the spelling like Jimi Hendrix. Catchy, easy to pronounce . . . then the capital E at the end. It just came to me."

"Hmm…when I hear it I think hip-hop. But that's just my first impression. What else you got?"

"Ron ReLillo."

"Can you spell that?"

I spelled it.

"Is there any special meaning behind it?"

"Well, you know, Don DeLillo has been such a huge inspiration to me. I thought…"

"Well, we don't need to decide this minute. Let's write them down and keep moving."

"I have a symbol, sort of like Prince used to use."

I found the page in my notebook and held it up for her to see.

"It's an ancient vampire cross and circle, but the cross is made with golf clubs and the circle is a golf ball with an eye. Naturally."

"Okay, I'll take a screenshot. Got it. But I do think we really need a name, something unique. Strong and lean, like your prose. Maybe we can switch to the symbol later."

"Makes complete sense. Another one I was thinking was Justin Time."

"Justin Time … hmm … Where have I heard that before? Isn't that a kids' show?"

"Is it? It might be… a coincidence. I was thinking because my vampire golfers are trapped in eternity."

"Why don't we add it to the list and keep brainstorming?"

"I have more. I knew this would be an issue someday. My name has always been so ordinary. On my worst days it's felt like a curse, like I'll always be ordinary. That's actually why I named one of my female vampire golfers Buffy, the one that always slices at key moments. You know, like she can't escape the curse of her name."

"What about Sam Buffy?"

"Sure, that could work."

THREE ARTICLES FOR *THE ONION*, SORT OF

(circa 2010, before The Onion ceased its print edition)

Article 1
Freelance Writer Exploits Crevice
in The Onion's Submission Policy
By Dirk Smeltzer

Sometimes all you need in life is the narrowest of crevices to gain a foothold. Once this sliver is secure, the territory can be exploited to build a niche.

At least that's the explanation fledgling humor writer Tim Miller gave as to why he spent so much time and energy this summer crafting pieces for *The Onion*.

The Onion, an award-winning publication that exclusively prints satire on current events, states in clear terms that freelance writing is not accepted, but that's not how this writer sees it.

"Their policy is utterly ambiguous," Miller said. "If you read between the lines, it's almost like they're begging for young, inexperienced writers seeking an audience."

"Take, for instance, the line, 'Unsolicited email attachments of any kind are not accepted and will be discarded/filtered immediately upon receipt.' That's pretty vague. OK—we get it. They don't like attachments. But are they discarding or filtering?"

He went on to point out that it's unclear whether they will immediately discard a submission or filter it into a "promising young writer" folder.

Miller works during the school year as a substitute teacher. Over the summer he freelances as a humor writer. Last summer he nearly completed a screenplay entitled, *No, You Can't Go to the Bathroom* about his experiences substitute teaching.

This summer he devoted himself wholeheartedly to writing mock journalism pieces for "America's Finest News Source."

It started the very first day of his summer vacation. As Miller explains, he suffered an excruciating morning of writer's block, staring disconsolately at his unfinished script.

"I felt like a deflated blimp," he said. "I was all excited to resume my journey toward becoming a humor writer, and I couldn't even get off the ground."

After a reflective pause, he continued.

"One of the reasons I got into teaching was so I could write during the summers, and suddenly I felt like my whole life was a complete waste of time. It was a similar agony to what James Joyce experienced while writing *Ulysses*."

Particularly vexing was the decision about whether the students would go to the bathroom at the end of the film, despite his rigid "no bathroom" policy.

"The ending tortured me all morning," he said.

In one ending, a defiant student goes to the bathroom, but it just "doesn't feel right," according to the writer.

"The other ending, which actually happened, is when I don't let the students leave the room for five full minutes after the dismissal bell, out of spite," he said. "But the ending is a little anticlimactic."

He didn't see a way out, until he took a break for lunch.

"I started singing while making a sandwich," he said of his lucid moment of inspiration. "It came to me out of nowhere, like the mysterious streams Hemingway talked about."

"Suddenly I was singing a song called, 'The Best Sandwich Ever.' It was definitely funny, like something that would be in *The Onion*."

That afternoon, he got to work.

Two months later, he had fifty different satirical news pieces that he considered "very strong." With one week left before the start of school, he investigated *The Onion's* submission policy. Despite the obvious language discouraging submissions, the writer remains convinced that opportunity is lurking behind the "opaque text."

When asked about the phrases "Any unsolicited résumés will be immediately discarded" and "editorial submissions of any kind are **not accepted**," Miller replied nonchalantly. "I'm not sending in a résumé to be their bitch. I don't get coffee for other people—I'm a writer. And my pieces aren't editorials. Editorial—what does that even mean? Say it three times fast and it sounds like a made-up word. Editorialeditorialeditorial."

The writer remained optimistic even when confronted with the Frequently Asked Questions portion of the website, which answers the question "How can I become a writer for *The Onion*?" with the following:

"All editorial content in *The Onion* is written by staff and there are currently no writing positions available.

"Any freelance material sent to *The Onion* will not be read and will not be returned.

"Should *The Onion* seek new talent in the future, a call for submissions will appear in our newspapers and on our website."

"Talk about wishy-washy," Miller explained. "They have to write that to discourage hacks. Bottom line, if you have a catchy headline, they'll read it. Take, for example, my piece about 'Past the Point of Passing Up Pasta.' How could you not read an article with a headline like that?"

Like anyone with a dream, Miller displays two critical qualities: determination and persistence.

"Or my piece about Al Roker from *The TODAY Show* getting fed up with the expression, 'Here's what's happening in your neck of the woods.' I mean, he says it every freaking day. That's gotta get old."

As for the script, Miller is uncertain when he will return to it. For now, he plans to continue to hone his satire writing for *The Onion*, sort of.

Amateur Songwriter Has Great Idea
for Song, Sandwich
By Dirk Smeltzer

Recreational singer-songwriter Gavin Pole recently found inspiration in, of all places, his kitchen. Which is surprising when you consider he is a worse cook than he is a musician, according to relatives. Yet there was no denying that a lightning bolt of creativity had struck the semi-bard on a recent Tuesday afternoon.

According to Pole, a college graduate waiting tables until he "figures things out," he was rummaging around for something to eat when the words seemed to come out of him. "I was scavenging through the fridge when, before I knew what was happening, I felt a surge of enthusiasm. And all of a sudden, I was making a sandwich I've never had before—and singing," Pole said. "It's hard to describe the process, but it was very spiritual."

Dissatisfied with his selection of lunchmeats, Pole discovered a Tupperware container with week-old leftover salmon. It smelled bad, but he put it in the microwave and the smell apparently improved after thirty seconds on medium heat. That's when he put a slice of mild, stiff cheddar on top of it and zapped it again for fifteen seconds. Next thing he knew, he was toasting a slightly hardened French baguette and singing tunelessly out loud, "This is going to be the best sandwich ever!"

"I knew instantly I had a chorus that people would sing along to, relate to," Pole said. "I mean, who hasn't gotten really excited about a sandwich?"

It was when he grabbed a plum tomato that he saw, out of the corner of his eye, the hummus. And that's when the song—and the sandwich—really took off.

"I wished I would've had a tape recorder going while I was slicing that tomato," Pole lamented.

He ad-libbed, in a style not unlike Jim Morrison's free-flowing wordplay, several verses while he sliced the tomato and slathered hummus on the baguette. When asked later what the verses were about, Pole showed a true amateur lack of confidence and replied diffidently, "My lunch, OK? I was excited about my lunch."

With the handle of his knife as a microphone, the tone-deaf singer belted out the chorus as if to an arena of rock fans: "This is going to be the best sandwich ever, the best sandwich ever, the best f*#kin ever!" Reaching for a crest of passion, as well as a mug to pour a diet root beer soda into, Pole followed his amateur songwriting instincts into the bridge of the song. Somberly and without rhythm, he went on a Dylanesque tangent about ice clinking and cracking, the soda a-fizzin' and a-snarlin'. The only thing missing was a harmonica fill that he has been meaning to learn.

Whether or not there were any side items, such as pretzels or chips, involved remains unclear, along with the future of the song. What is clear is that what happened next will belong forever in amateur songwriting folklore as a major "coulda-been."

He took a napkin, walked down the hall, and, unfortunately for the amateur songwriter, sat down in front of ESPN to eat his lunch.

He hummed several bars out of key in between the first few mouthfuls, but apparently hunger and speculation about NFL coaching changes superseded the sandwich's role as sorta-musical muse.

"It was a good sandwich. Not the best ever, but good," Pole said later. "And it gave me a great idea for a song. But, wow, I just can't get over how many coaches get axed every off-season."

Pole has, several times, nearly performed original and cover songs on open mic night at local taverns. He has no immediate plans to perform, but reports are that he practices nearly every day.

"He plays guitar every afternoon and it drives me nuts," next-door neighbor Uma Krishnan said. "Usually, I've just put my two-year-old down for a nap, and he starts—I wouldn't call it playing music, because it's more like noise. Sometimes, I get so irritated that I bang on the wall. He usually stops."

Article 3
Not Past the Point of Passing Up Pasta
By Dirk Smeltzer

Considering the two college roommates, Don Wagner and Richard Schneidecki, had eaten pasta for dinner for nine consecutive nights, there was nothing unusual about the penne pasta with chopped up hot dogs that Wagner prepared one Thursday evening.

It's certainly not unusual for college students to try to save money on a grocery bill. Yet, the night in question was the beginning of something quite unusual indeed—an unusual question.

"I remember we were watching this movie with Arnold Schwarzenegger," Schneidecki, or Schni-dukeduke, as his friends call him, began. "I don't know what it's called, but it's a terrible movie. He was in Columbia and like a thousand guys with a thousand machine guns couldn't hit him. It was ridiculous. The plot was awful. I don't really remember what it was about.

"Oh," Schni-dukeduke continued, as Wagner raised his eyebrows. "Sorry. The unusual question. Well, we were sitting there watching the movie, when all of a sudden Don turned to me and asked if I was 'past the point.'

"I thought he was talking about the movie," Schni-dukeduke went on. "I remember now that Arnold's wife and kid were killed by a bomb by this terrorist. He went on the warpath to get this terrorist—that's why he was in Columbia."

At this point Wagner did a mock slap on his roommate's forehead, reminding Schni-dukeduke to get back on track.

"That's my bad. It's just that the movie was that awful. Anyway, before I could change the channel, Don said, 'No, not the movie. Are you past the point of passing up pasta?'"

There's really only one answer to such a question, Schni-dukeduke pointed out. "No, of course not. I'm *not* past the point of passing up pasta!"

To which Wagner responded that he wasn't past the point of passing up pasta, either.

That was almost a month ago. Now, they haven't been past the point of passing up pasta for almost forty consecutive nights. What began as a joke to make light of limited economical resources has grown into a notorious conversation on campus.

"Penne, angel hair, lasagna, spaghetti, macaroni, fettuccine, linguine, ravioli, farfalle, rigatoni, tortellini, gnocchi," Schni-dukeduke listed. "Some I don't even know the names of. Like the round, wheel shaped one. We've done them all. Sometimes we have sauce, sometimes we use butter or just parmesan cheese. Once, we made this strange casserole with tuna fish and pickles.

"Then, this past week, we basically ate ramen noodles," Schni-dukeduke said.

"Ahelluvalotta pasta," Wagner added.

The meals have been supplemented with a box of brownies sent by Schni-dukeduke's mom. Beyond that, the two juniors, who have yet to declare their majors, have no plans to pass the point of passing up pasta any time soon.

Further, Schni-dukeduke has almost completed his training to become a server at DiAngelo's, a local Italian restaurant, and will soon begin to collect more significant wages. Yet, he doesn't think his earnings will change their eating habits.

"I eat at work and then take food home after a training session," Schni-dukeduke said. "So between the restaurant and our streak, I eat a lot of pasta."

"Ahelluvalot," Wagner added.

When asked what would happen first, getting "past the point of passing up pasta" or declaring a major, the two students seemed unsure.

"*Collateral Damage!*" Schni-dukeduke suddenly blurted out. "That was the name of the movie."

The Wild and the Innocent, hosted by Jim Rotolo, airs on Friday evenings on Sirius XM's E Street Radio. The show starts at 6 p.m. EST. But since I live in Southern California, the program comes on the air at 3 p.m. PST, right about the time I am pulling out of my school's parking lot and bracing for the traffic heading north on I-5. Friday traffic. Friday. Traffic.

My physical and mental state at this hour usually ranges from worn down to sheer exhaustion to questioning Man's place in the universe. My expression in the rearview mirror usually says something along the lines of "Holy hell!" And that's before I even pull onto the highway. There's a dull buzz in my head, and my lower lip, jaw, and chin are all—I can assure you—quite, quite rigid.

When I first discovered Jim Rotolo's show, I thought I had found the perfect balm for my end-of-the-week stressies. Each week, Jim selects a different theme, like Best Opener, Song You've Never Heard Live, or Songs for Greatest Hits Volume II. People call in, they chat with Jim, he plays a couple of tunes, and the cycle repeats.

The first time I listened to the show, I caught a live "Badlands" followed by an acoustic "Factory Song." The music did what music can do: It lifted me up out of my doldrums and stomped out all my little pathetic whimpers.

I soon fell into a routine of listening to the show every Friday. Not only did it cure my lumpy stone face, but it also provided relief from a curious tendency I had to flip around between stations on the drive home. It seemed the more tired I was, the less anything on the radio sounded appealing. In the morning, drinking coffee, I could listen to myriad stations with delight, familiar and unfamiliar alike. On the way home—especially on Fridays—every channel was like a hot potato.

Until I stumbled upon Jim's show. As I tuned in each week, I noticed Jim had an unusually good rapport with callers. Clearly, the show has a following, and it isn't just because of Springsteen's music. Jim, as host, exudes both a profound depth of knowledge regarding everything Springsteen and extensive radio experience.

As the months passed, I noticed that some people called in regularly. I began to suspect that Jim's following might be due to his extraordinary, even preternatural, ability to engage in Small Talk. His radio personality is outgoing and sympathetic. He is part friend, part Bruce superfan, part psychologist, and part host. Call 877-70-BRUCE, request a song, share a story, and get a dose of empathy.

He could shoot the bull with just about anyone and it never seemed forced or strained. Perfect strangers and Jim could chew the fat like old neighbors.

I would think of Jim Rotolo when my own Small Talk seemed inadequate, forced, or insincere. I began to study his Small Talk, as an apprentice studies a master.

I'm not sure when it happened. It was gradual. Subtle. Furtive. But then it was there and I had to confront it: Jim's Small Talk was irritating the shit out of me. I could change the channel for a full song on Pearl Jam Radio, come back, and still hear Jim batting it around with Susan in Winnipeg about Bruce never playing Winnipeg.

I realize that it's part of the show, part of the community of Bruce fans, calling in and chatting and rehashing old Bruce memories. I get it. It's a forum that's part of *The Wild & the Innocent's* format. It's *The Wild & the Innocent* WITH Jim Rotolo. It's what makes Jim Jim and The Show The Show. It's endearing. Humanizing. The Show isn't just about the music. It's also about the fans and their stories and their interpretations and what Bruce means to them.

It's necessary. But every once in a while, it really isn't. In fact, it's completely unnecessary when I need my Boss Fix to break through the crust of work and stress and all that builds up each week. It's like a crack dealer chatting about his cousin's high school volleyball game with an addict that just needs the drug now.

Not only did the Small Talk become irritating; it also, occasionally, without warning, veered into Big Talk. Recently a woman, out of nowhere, brought up how she was diagnosed with MS and how, when she received the diagnosis, her husband left her. Jim, ever the pro, handled this news delicately. He asked questions that were appropriate without probing. Then he steered away, back to Bruce, then came back and finished the conversation tactfully, acknowledging her pain and heartache.

But even the master wasn't perfect. The more I listened, the more I found reassurance that Jim is like me: fallible in the Art of Small Talk. Everyone, even a professional DJ, occasionally falls flat in conversation.

Here is an example: Ryan from Stanton called in to dedicate a song to his girlfriend's daughter on her ninth birthday. Ryan went on forever about how Bruce calls up young girls to sing with him on stage. He then rambled on, something about Taylor Swift and the Ellen DeGeneres Show.

After his blathering, Jim asked, "Are you doing anything special for the daughter?"

Ryan, sounding offended, responded, "No, I thought I would leave it to her mom. You know, give them some space and all."

Then, palpable all the way in San Diego: silence. Awwwkkkwwwaaarrrddd silence lasting multiple seconds.

Jim muttered, then hesitated, at which point Ryan asked if an upcoming show was sold out. Jim did not happen to know, off the top of his head, this information which is readily available online. Call Ticketmaster was his advice "to anyone wanting to know." Thanks Jim! How much does the stadium hold? Ryan wanted to know. Again, Jim did not have the information on or off or near the top of his head, considering the pit, the field seats, and behind the stage. Cringeworthy indeed. At this point Jim, struggling to end the conversation gracefully, said, "Thanks Ryan, I'm going to have to let you run." As if Ryan had anywhere to be on his girlfriend's daughter's birthday!

*

The following is inspired by Jim Rotolo. Thanks for lifting me up on Fridays. I will try to be patient with the Small Talk. Hope you don't mind a little spoof. (The protagonist, based loosely on Jim, might be, in fact, his antithesis.)

Boss Radio

Satellite Radio Office
New York, NY

"Hi Frank. Thanks for coming in."

"Sure. I always do what the suits say."

Frank slumps down in a chair. He is wearing sunglasses and a wrinkled Stone Pony T-shirt.

"I presume you know what this is about."

"I have an idea. You guys will say that I stepped on some line. You'll tell me not to step on the line again. And I gwin weal wide wike a good widdle boy."

"Sorry if that's how you feel. We at corporate feel very strongly that you're doing an excellent job on Boss Radio. Your show, *Radio Nowhere,* is one of our most popular."

"Whoop-de-doo."

"We recognize your skills as an asset to our programming."

"Well, at least someone is recognizing my ass."

"Frank. Let's keep things civil. I think we can reach an understanding. We can't have any more of what happened during last Friday's show, which is the third incident in as many months."

Frank sighs.

"Would you mind taking off your sunglasses?"

Frank takes a prolonged breath, exhaling through his nose. He removes his shades, cleans them using his Stone Pony T-shirt, and reaffixes them to the bridge of his nose.

The executive studies Frank for a moment, staring into his own reflection in the aviator shades. He shifts his head, a visual indicator of a new approach.

"I understand that you are currently going through a divorce."

"Yeppers."

"And I also understand that you are in the midst of a battle over custody of your two children."

"That's correct, for eight hundred dollars." Then he pitches his voice up an octave and says, "I'll take 'Staring at an Asshole' for one thousand, Alex."

"And it's obvious, by your appearance, smell, and behavior, that the substance abuse that we've previously discussed and outlined as unacceptable has not changed in any way, thus violating the terms of the probationary status of your contract."

"It's a Daily Douchebag Double!"

"Before I offer you the terms of your final opportunity to be a broadcaster on satellite radio, you might want to listen to your own voice on the following recording and then decide who the asshole is."

The executive clicks play.

"Let's go to Dan in New Jersey. Thanks for calling into *Radio Nowhere*, keeping people alive out there. Today's topic is, 'Most Underrated Bruce Song.' We're hearing a lot of rarities today. Deep stuff. We've heard a lot off *Human Touch* and *Tracks*, albums that don't get enough credit, to be sure. We just heard 'Reason to Believe' from the *Nebraska* album. Thanks to Steve in Buffalo who hit me up on Twitter. So, Dan, what is your most underrated Bruce song?"

"Hey Frank. Thanks for taking my call."

"You bet."

"Love the show."

"Thank you."

"Is it raining in New York?"

"Not right now, but we might get some showers this evening."

"It's raining in Jersey right now. Buckets."

"Yeah, I think I saw some stuff moving through the area on the Doppler."

"We're getting drenched."

"Well, hopefully you don't have anywhere to go and you can just tune in to Boss Radio."

"I ain't got nowhere to be. Most Fridays I like to sit back with a few cold beverages and listen to your show."

"Cool. Well, do you have an underrated Bruce song on your mind, something you love to crank up, and your friends don't get why you love it but it touches a nerve?"

"You bet I do. This song always makes me want to howl at the moon. Whenever I hear it—Oh, shit. I think I left my windows down. One second, let me run and make sure."

Frank utters a few muffled words. "I need a cold one myself" is audible. There are about five seconds of dead air.

"I guess it's raining in Jersey," Frank says.

More dead air.

"Hey, sorry. I ran out to grab some beef jerky before the rain started and thought I left my windows down."

"It's all good. So how about helping me keep people alive out there with an underrated Bruce song?"

"I didn't though."

Frank's tone crashes like an angry wave. "You didn't have a song?"

"No, I do. I didn't leave my windows down."

"Oh. That's a relief to millions of listeners."

"Everyone can relate to that feeling of having your windows down in a storm, right?"

"I'm sure most people can relate to that, yes. Now how about that tune? A Bruce song that doesn't get enough credit."

"OK. My most overrated song is 'Born to Run.'"

"'Born to Run?' *Over*-rated?"

"That song blows me away every time."

"Dan, did you mean to say that you think 'Born to Run' is an overrated song, which is a ludicrous proposition, or are you confused by the meaning of the terms 'overrated' and 'underrated'?"

"I think 'Born to Run' kicks ass and you can't play it enough on Bruce Radio."

A loud noise, like a forehead slamming against the microphone, is heard, followed by the F word.

"I don't think 'Born to Run' is in any danger of being underrated, a term which you clearly don't understand the meaning of. In fact, I think you've got a serious case of windows down in your own head and too much rain is washing away—"

A faint voice speaks in the background.

"No. We are not playing 'Born to Run' on a show about *under*-rated Bruce songs. This guy is a grade A moron and probably illiterate. We're talking about one of his most popular—"

There's a clicking noise, followed by five seconds of silence, before the intro to "Born to Run" begins:

In the day we sweat it out on the streets . . .

The executive presses pause. He is about to say something, then holds his tongue and extends the document to be signed. Frank signs it and walks out. The executive shakes his head. He starts to crease the paper when his eye catches the phrase that Frank wrote instead of his signature. His expression is one of mild disgust, as if pondering the feasibility of the intimate and solitary act Frank had suggested on the signature line.

The Summer of LeBran: May

The following articles from the Riverview Tribune chronicle the end of the 2018 NSPA Playoffs and the beginning of the 2018 Pizza Delivery Free Agent Signing Period.

May 27, 2018

LeBran's the Man
By Tom Witherspoon

Delivering another pizza for the ages, James LeBran dropped 46 pizzas on the suburb of Riverview and preserved his reign atop the Eastern Conference of the Northern Suburban Pizzeria Association for at least one more night. With Il-Forno's Pizzeria a driver short, and veteran and former delivery All-Star Matt Harrigan out with a strained timing belt, LeBran once again rose to the occasion in a climactic night of pie delivery. Il-Forno's out-delivered Piero's 109-99 to force a Night 7 in the Eastern Suburbs Finals.

LeBran, delivering pizzas for possibly his final night in an Il-Forno's uniform, added 17 appetizers and 11 salads while driving for all but two minutes of Saturday's marathon.

With rumors swirling about his pizza future, LeBran focused on what he does best: delivery.

"Greatness," Il-Forno's owner Debbie Lake said. "Gave it his all. We needed that, especially with Matt going down. He delivered and carried us home, as usual."

The Pizza King is not dead, and he still has a chance to compete in his eighth straight North Suburban Pizzeria Association Finals. If he does, and Judy's Pizzeria overcomes Nino's, it would set up a fourth straight Finals matchup between the rival pizzerias.

"It feels good to be able to deliver for another night," said LeBran, who had his seventh 40-pizza night of the

Pizzeria Playoffs. "Like I've always said, Game 7 is the best two words in pizza delivery. That and 'big tip.' We should relish the opportunity and have fun with it."

The series will have a fitting conclusion on Sunday—Piero's was 26-0 this season on Sundays. They were especially dominant during football season.

"Our goal is to be able to compete for a championship, and what more could you ask for?" LeBran said. "If you said to me at the beginning of the delivery season that we only needed one match to make the Finals, we'd take it."

JR Cresham added 20 pizzas and Bernie Harrigan 14 for Il-Forno's after losing brother Matt Harrigan in the first rush when he flew over a speed bump and knocked his timing belt out.

Terry Pogofski paced Piero's, now 10-16 on Saturday nights, with 28 pizzas. Brady Brown had 27. "We haven't figured out a way to handle the waves of rushes that Saturdays bring," Pogofski said. "Unlike Sundays with halftimes and kickoffs, Saturdays are unpredictable."

Piero's was still within seven pizzas in the final thirty minutes before closing time when LeBran made consecutive triple deliveries. He punctuated the second by pounding his chest with both fists and screaming at the perplexed couple receiving the pizzas.

"I've never seen a pizza delivery boy so excited," Mr. Lindgren of Pine Street commented.

"I thought maybe the size of our tip offended him," Mrs. Lindgren said.

For good measure, LeBran added an Italian beef in the final fifteen minutes before closing time and was taken off the road to a rousing ovation from cooks, delivery boys, and the phone girl Crystal Paige chanting "Il-Forno's in 7!"

"Just a lot of heart, a lot of grit, being resilient," LeBran said.

Piero's improbable run through the pizzeria postseason without injured delivery stars Kai Ree and Howard Gordon will now focus on Sunday, beginning with the lunch rush, where they have delivered with more intensity and togetherness to loyal customers eager to see an 18th banner raised to the rafters of the storied pizzeria.

"It's not going to be a party," Pogofski said. "We've got to come out ready to get our nose bloody and our mouth bloody. We've got to come out ready to fight. You've got to find a way, whatever it takes."

The real possibility that LeBran was delivering his final night for Il-Forno's hung over the contest—and the entire city of Riverview—in the hours leading up to opening. Everyone had an opinion regarding what LeBran will do next, and that discussion filled the pizza talk airwaves, bars, and barbershops.

The 33-year-old has said several times since returning home in 2014 that he wants to retire with Il-Forno's, but customers are uneasy because he can opt out of his $12-an-hour-plus-tip contract this summer and test free agency.

And of course, he left once before, in 2010, bolting for Barnaby's.

LeBran has said that he'll sit down with his family after the season ends to plot his next move. He's already being courted by Sarpino's, Buffo's, and Ferentino's, who can only dream of adding him to their delivery rosters.

For now, he's going to work for Il-Forno's.

Piero's owner Steve Bradley praised LeBran for his consistency and ability to exceed expectations. "Nobody else has what he has on his shoulders delivering pie," he said. "I think that the way in which he's done that, and all of the years now that he's made the Finals and gone deep in the Pizzeria Playoffs—it's unbelievable."

May 28, 2018

James LeBran Wills Ramshackle Il-Forno's
Back to the Finals
By Tom Witherspoon

James LeBran honked at Piero's as he drove past. A street sign obscured by a lane closure couldn't stop him. When his last large cheese of the evening was ruled good, LeBran released a scream that the stunned road workers could only marvel at. The thin crusted dagger in Il-Forno's 87-79 pizza coronation in Game 7 of the Eastern Riverview Pizza Finals is one Riverview residents will remember for years to come.

LeBran delivered once again.

"It's what's been asked of me from this pizzeria," LeBran said. "I'm the leader of this pizza restaurant and I'm going to give what I got."

The Pizza Finals start Thursday night with either Judy's or Nino's and, improbably, Il-Forno's will be there.

Delivery boys Matt Harrigan, Bernie Harrigan, and JR Cresham. Phone girl Crystal Paige. Cooks Maximino Jimenez and Geraldo Cortez. Owner Debbie Lake. Assistant manager Trevor Schmidt. They are once again Eastern Conference of the North Suburban Pizzeria Association champions, all thanks to LeBran's dominance. He finished with 35 pizzas, 15 salads, and nine appetizers while delivering the entire night. He will deliver in the Pizza Finals for the eighth straight year.

"He's unbelievable," Piero's owner Steve Bradley said. "I don't think he made a single wrong turn. He does it at this level, with the pressure, with the scrutiny. Doesn't matter. Our goal going into the series was to make him exert as much energy as humanly possible . . . but he still delivered 35 pizzas. It's a joke."

Il-Forno's needed every ounce of his kingly reign, because young Piero's did not go quietly.

Piero's had been labeled as too inexperienced and too injured to make a lasting dent in these Pizzeria Playoffs, let alone to earn the Eastern Riverview Pizza crown. And yet the customers who raged down Legends Way into Piero's on Sunday, their stomachs growling inside the restaurant, believed.

"They have good pizza," one customer said. "It's the crust. It's very crispy."

And most of all, the drivers and staff of Piero's believed. They will now take their belief, along with their leftovers, into the off-season.

May 29, 2018

Long Shots: Odds Against Il-Forno's
in NSPA Finals vs. Judy's
By Tom Witherspoon

The odds are longer than a Stephen Hurry triple delivery, Kevin Durade's spoilers, or Thomas Clay's catalog of speeding tickets.

James LeBran and Il-Forno's are being given little—or no—chance of winning their fourth straight NSPA Finals matchup against Judy's Pizzeria, who have been installed by Riverview bookmakers as the heaviest favorite in the past sixteen years.

Wanna bet?

Judy's are 12-pizza favorites to win Thursday's Game 1, the largest spread in a Finals game since 1991.

Il-Forno's owner Debbie Lake isn't blinking.

"We're all focused on winning a championship," Lake said Tuesday during a lull in the lunch hour. "We delivered our best pizza going into the playoffs. We've gotten better and better throughout the course of the playoffs. Our main focus and our main objective is to win a championship, so

100

we can't worry about what the outside guys are saying and who's being picked. We know what we have here and what we're trying to do."

Il-Forno's vs. Judy's, Part IV: an unexpected conclusion to an unpredictable season.

Lake said All-Star driver Matt Harrigan's car remains in the shop with a timing belt issue and his status for the series opener is in question. Harrigan sat out Il-Forno's Game 7 win vs. Piero's on Sunday after suffering the timing belt mishap in Game 6, driving too fast over a speed bump.

Harrigan was replaced in the driving lineup by his brother, veteran Bernie Harrigan, who stepped up and delivered 19 pizzas as Il-Forno's completed their comeback after trailing 2-0 and 3-2 in the series.

Matt Harrigan is expected back for Game 1 of the Finals. Lake needs his experience against Judy's who, like Il-Forno's, rallied to win the Western Conference Finals by taking Game 7 vs. Nino's.

There was a moment when it looked as if both Il-Forno's and Nino's could miss the Finals.

That moment passed quickly.

"They've been tested. We've been tested," Lake said. "They've been to Game 7s. We've been to Game 7s. We've won championships and they've won championships, so they understand what it takes and they knew what it took."

Since the pizza delivery playoffs opened, Il-Forno's has embraced the "Whatever it Takes" mantra that began as a catchy organizational slogan and morphed into a way of survival.

Il-Forno's has twice been pushed to seven games, overcome car troubles, and gotten much-needed contributions to ease the burden on LeBran from drivers Cresham and Bernie Harrigan, and phone girl Crystal Paige.

In this series when every pizza will be magnified, Lake will count on the veteran staff members who have been around since Il-Forno's first met Judy's in the 2015 Finals:

assistant manager Trevor Schmidt, cook Maximino Jimenez, and driver Matt Harrigan.

And because they won a championship in 2016 together, the core four of LeBran, Harrigan, Schmidt, and Jimenez share something special.

"Just having these guys here who have been through it, been through the tough times, been through the great times as well—this is a bond that can't be broken," Lake said. "It reminds me a lot of people I worked with back in the day when I was a hostess at Baker's Square and we won the Omelet Trophy—something about winning a championship with those guys that you will never forget, and it's a bond that can't be broken."

While Harrigan has been solid, Schmidt and Jimenez haven't always come through this season for Il-Forno's.

One of the streakiest assistant managers in the league, Schmidt has had prolonged slumps. Jimenez, who has missed time during the pizza playoffs with a nagging thumb injury after cutting himself dicing onions, wasn't a factor until Lake started him in Game 7 of the first round vs. Pizano's.

Lake never lost faith in either her cook or her assistant manager. It's a trust that can't be measured.

"I'm always going to stick behind my guys," Lake said. "Even when they're struggling, I have confidence and a belief that when we need those guys, and we call on those guys, they'll be ready and they'll deliver pie. You've seen that throughout the course of the playoffs this year and you've seen it the last three years, that those guys are up for the challenge. They rise to the occasion. And just because a cook is not cooking well, or a manager is slipping, you can't give up on a guy.

"You gotta give those guys a chance, especially when you've been there before with them and you know who they are."

Unlike the past three Finals, Lake won't have Kai Ree, who was traded to Piero's last summer.

The All-Star driver was Il-Forno's not-so-secret weapon, the one they turned to in order to spell LeBran and keep Judy's off-balance.

"He allowed us to deliver one-on-one when orders were mismatched, and nobody can stop him one-on-one," Lake said. "We're gonna miss that, so we're going to have to take a different style of pizza delivery without him being here."

Now that's a safe bet.

May 31, 2018

Judy's Withstands 51 Pizzas from LeBran to Win Game 1 of the NSPA Finals
By Tom Witherspoon

Judy's somehow withstood James LeBran's latest brilliance on the NSPA stage.

A costly blunder by JR Cresham and a disputed traffic violation involving LeBran himself sure helped.

Steph Hurry delivered 29 pizzas and Judy's capitalized on Cresham's mistake that sent the contest into overtime, overcoming a 51-pizza performance by LeBran to beat Il-Forno's 124-114 in Game 1 on Thursday Night.

The game nearly over, LeBran jawed with both Hurry and Thomas Clay at a red light, then Il-Forno's phone girl Crystal Paige called up Judy's and got into it with phone girl Draymonda Grey, resulting in the Il-Forno's receptionist being disqualified with 2.6 seconds left.

LeBran was in utter disbelief as regulation ended stunningly: When Bernie Harrigan left to deliver two free orders of garlic rolls with 4.7 seconds left, he dropped the second bag of rolls. JR Cresham pulled in, secured the fallen rolls, and ran inside to LeBran, apparently thinking Il-Forno's had the lead.

"He thought it was over. He thought we were up," owner Lake said.

Yet Cresham insisted that he knew the score.

Phone girl Grey figured Cresham was simply looking for LeBran, saying, "I would've looked for LeBran, too."

"I found the bag of garlic rolls on the street," Cresham said. "I didn't know Bernie dropped them. I just thought that LeBran would want some. Usually food that gets dropped or messed up belongs to the drivers."

A delivered garlic roll would have meant victory. Instead, OT.

And why not? Both these pizzerias were pushed to their limits in seven-game conference finals.

"I can't talk about a situation that way because I do some dumb stuff when I'm delivering pizzas," Judy's driver Kevin Durade said. "I don't know what was going through JR's head. He made a great pickup of the bag of garlic rolls and gave them an opportunity to win."

Game 2 is Sunday night.

"We've got to move on," LeBran said. "This night is over and done with. We had opportunities."

Both Hurry and Clay had five triple deliveries for Judy's. Matt Harrigan returned from a strained timing belt to provide a big boost for Il-Forno's with 21 pizzas and 13 salads.

Everyone expects another wild one with so much talent on both sides.

"It was a crazy night," Hurry said. "The Finals, man, anything is liable to happen."

"So, your parents are getting a divorce?"

"Yes."

"And how does that make you feel?"

She shrugged and tossed a piece of gum into her mouth.

He stared at her. She threw in another piece. He kept staring and stroked his beard. She looked away and then looked back to see his fingers playing with the whiskers on his neck, the part where he had shaved maybe two or three days ago.

Finally, he said, "Surely you must have some opinion on it. Remember, this is a safe place. You can be honest and share your feelings. Nothing you say leaves these four walls."

"It is what it is."

He stroked his beard again, like he was petting a cat. "I see," he said. "Oftentimes teenagers are angry at one or both of their parents when they get a divorce. Are you angry at them?"

"No."

"Disappointed?"

"No."

"Do you feel that they don't love you?"

"No."

"Do you feel responsible, like it was in any way your fault?"

"No."

He began to rub the tip of his beard, which was very orange, as if he was sharpening it.

"Research suggests that most teenagers harbor feelings of resentment and guilt, which fester and lead to some, shall we say, rather unsavory behavior, like poor academics or drug use."

"I don't do drugs and I have straight A's," she said.

"Do you think that your grades will bring your parents back together?"

"No. It's over."

He narrowed his eyes and brushed both sides of his beard, as if he was trying to get sand out of it but couldn't. "Sometimes my patients will bottle up feelings, try to avoid them, and eventually lash out."

"Not me." She blew a big bubble, and it popped as he leaned in.

"Alcohol?"

"I don't drink."

"Sexual activity?"

"I have a boyfriend."

"Yes . . ."

"But we haven't done it, if that's what you mean. He's pretty religious."

"Most kids of divorce report having problems in their own relationships. Do you worry about this, that it may affect your current relationship?"

"No. My boyfriend's parents are divorced, too. He's been pretty supportive."

"Thoughts of leaving home or running away?"

"No."

"Thoughts of hurting someone, or even yourself?"

"No."

"Aggression?"

She shook her head.

"Anxiety?"

"Not really."

"Not even a hint?"

"Nope."

"What about your little brother? You will have to take care of him, take on more responsibility."

"He's a sweet kid. It's no hassle."

He was scratching now like an insect had burrowed into his chin.

"Has your mom or dad used you as a confidant in any way? Telling you any secrets or information, asking you to spy on the other?"

"Actually, yes."

His eyes widened.

"My dad asked me to watch closely how my mom folds the sheets, the fitted ones, so that I could do that for him."

"The fitted sheets?"

"Yes. My dad said he has never been able to fold them properly—especially the elastic corners—and that my mom is really good at it."

"C'MON NOW BLAST IT!" He suddenly shouted, gripping his cheeks with each hand. "Surely there must be some pain you are feeling? Some level of depression or hurt or insecurity? A shred of antisocial behavior or withdrawal, or even a slightly destructive act? How about susceptibility to negative peer influence? Give me something!"

"My parents are getting divorced. They don't love each other, but they'll always love my brother and me."

"Fine." He leaned back and gave his beard a final sweep. "Tell me about the sheets again. Go very slowly."

DISPELLING THE MISCONCEPTIONS SURROUNDING THE OTHER WOODY ALLEN SCANDAL

Hachette dropped Woody Allen's memoir. Amazon backed out of a four-movie deal. His most recent film isn't being released in the US. What's going on?

Sure, the cloud of suspicion and scandal has followed him for thirty years. Allegations. Sexual assault. Adopted daughters. Investigations. It's all rather sordid and unpleasant.

If only some other scandal could rush in, like a breath of fresh air. If only some yellow journalist would usher in, for lack of a better term, a real doozy. And might it have something to do with the fact that, as a young man, a certain Heywood Allen was expelled from both New York University and the City College of New York? And was involved in communist activities!

Now blow, ye idiot winds of yellow journalism! Blow!

For the first time, the public has access to information suggesting that "Heywood" Allen's expulsions were not merely a result of poor grades. According to a bowling team from Greenwich Village called A Small Group of Literary Scholars, the case of Mr. Allen's dismissal from both institutions is a dramatic and shocking tale that has been concealed in the National Archives for more than fifty years.

A Small Group of Literary Scholars (which later became the Insatiables when team captain Brad Milovich quit over philosophical differences, including the view of character being secondary to plot and whether to roll the ball straight or curvy) discovered classified documents after a quarterfinals match against a team known as the Set-Ups, who were actually FBI agents working clandestinely on a drug sting. One Jude Byanski, a rookie on the Set-Ups, became so inebriated during the course of the match that he left behind his bag, glove, ball, and surveillance equipment, plus a sheath of what was at first thought to be scratch paper from an FBI recycling bin used to calculate scoring averages. The Insatiables lost the match, but they, and the world, have quite possibly gained valuable insight into the history of a great American comedian.

According to these documents, a New York University communications professor named Max Shulman noticed young Allen's left-leaning tendencies early on. For example, he filed a complaint with the dean claiming that this "Heywood" Allen refused to sit during lectures and instead leaned against the left wall. This incited students who disagreed with Allen to lean against the right wall. It got so bad that nobody in the lecture hall would sit down. Moreover, a student, presumably Heywood, would surreptitiously tilt the projector to the left. His fingerprints were all over it. (Later it came out that he was in the AV crew.) Towards the end of the semester, Professor Shulman withdrew from the class and filed a grievance with the teachers' union claiming intolerable teaching conditions. In the grievance he lamented handprints on the windows, projector alignment, and an insidious conspiracy (presumably led by Heywood) to move his podium six inches to the left before every class. As evidence, Shulman submitted a picture taken halfway through the semester where he was standing behind a podium in the 14th Street subway station.

Apparently, with the podium prank, Heywood had leaned too far.

These practices put Mr. Allen on the school's radar, but it was his involvement with an intramural badminton team, the Red Birdies, that officially put Heywood on a government watch list for communist activities. The Red Birdies refused to have a team captain, claiming that all Red Birdies were equal. Further, they refused to wear numbers. This caused quite a stir and confused the officials overseeing the intramural tournament, particularly those in charge of monitoring substitutions. The Red Birdies went on to win the tournament, only to have their victory—and trophy—stripped due to perceived substitution violations. The team's members protested the decision to the student body governing board on the grounds that the entire tournament became a fetter between the superstructure and the base. Since none of the five members of the student board had ever heard the word *fetter* before, the case was thrown out.

Heywood was so distraught over this ruling that he later broke into the dormitory room of Robert Benchley, the captain of the newly appointed championship team THE FEATHERS, and stole back the trophy. It is not known whether THE FEATHERS used all capital letters as a coincidence or as an endorsement of capitalism.

The trophy was later found abandoned at the student union, where authorities apprehended Heywood for stealing cheese fries in the student cafeteria. It was his fifth offense of stealing cafeteria food—always cheese fries— which, according to the student Code of Conduct, dictated an immediate expulsion.

In the fall of 1953, the scene shifted from NYU to the City College of New York, but the shadow of controversy once again followed young "Heywood" onto campus.

He became active in student government, ostensibly motivated to improve the vocabulary of college student governing bodies. In his campaign to become student body president, he lost to Theodore Roosevelt's grandson, Charles "Chucky" Roosevelt.

Irked by perceived favoritism (and the number of Roosevelt grandchildren enrolled in the college), Heywood soon initiated a coup to remove Chucky Roosevelt as president. There was widespread dissatisfaction amongst the student body over having to pay for condiments in the student cafeteria. Heywood uncovered a contract that Roosevelt had finagled between the college and an undisclosed US condiment corporation revealing, amongst other shady undertakings, that to increase profits the corporation had inserted the PEEL HERE label in an area not engineered for peeling.

The coup was an unbridled success. In place of Chucky Roosevelt, Heywood installed as virtual director Shah Mohammed Pavlovi, a sophomore he had befriended while playing metaphysical billiards in the psychology building's recreational room.

It should be noted that during this period at City College "Heywood" changed his name to "Chéwood," (perhaps adding another layer of appellation subterfuge) and regularly donned a plain green army jacket, a beret, and a goatee.

City College, along with its president George S. Kaufman, supported the Shah's student government in its struggle for universal, free, all-you-can-carry condiments in student cafeterias across campus. He invalidated the fraudulent contract with the undisclosed US corporation and signed on with the Anglo-Persian Oil Company, which also sold condiments. Furthermore, the college assisted the Shah in creating the SQUIRTS, an elite secret police force intended to quell any condiment opposition.

Finally—and most brazenly— City College cooperated with the Shah's student government for the development of an Iranian laminator plant in exchange for two dozen new laminators to be used in faculty lounges across campus in what came to be known as the "Mayonnaise for Peaceful Laminating" program. It is unclear how Chéwood established a connection to an Iranian laminator dealer. Presumably, the Shah "knew a guy."

The CIA installed several covert operatives in the SQUIRTS to monitor his activities, unbeknownst to Chéwood.

Soon the Shah's—and indirectly Chéwood's—support from the student body began to erode in the face of a student cafeteria workers' union strike. A young political science major and labor organizer (none other than Bippy Roosevelt, Chucky's brother) led them out on strike. The free condiments had led to a reduction of wages and therefore a disgruntled energy amongst the workers, which Bippy harnessed to initiate the strike. There was no food served in student cafeterias for a week leading up to what came to be known as "Thanks-but-no-Thanksgiving break."

After Thanks-but-no-Thanksgiving, the cafeterias reopened with the SQUIRTS working as scabs. The pressure continued to mount between the student body and Roosevelt's striking cafeteria workers as negotiations continued. In response to packets of ketchup being stashed under parked car tires—leaving the appearance of blood in the streets—City College provided the SQUIRTS with condiment dispensers.

According to intel gained shortly before one covert agent went quiet (with laryngitis), Chéwood considered deposing the Shah and ruling the student body himself with an iron fist. He abandoned this plan when he learned that the fist he had purchased at a flea market was actually made of zinc.

The fuse was finally lit when the Shah was exposed as someone who played with puppets, igniting the student body in a red, explosive overthrow of the government and the SQUIRTS on pasta night.

Behind the scenes, President Kaufman instantly withdrew his support of "Mayonnaise for Peaceful Laminating." (The US government has since worked to prevent Iran from having a laminator-exporting program.)

Chucky Roosevelt adroitly resumed his position as head of the student government. Ironically, the condiment dispensers were later used by the administration to justify abolishing the cafeteria union on grounds that it posed a clear and present danger to the students, who kept slipping. The SQUIRTS disbanded, with many of the lead members turning their attention to dorm and parking lot security.

The ultimate blow that drove Chéwood from his left-leaning ways was when he announced that the vocabulary of the student government had stagnated and the governing board members collectively returned a blank stare. He shaved his goatee on the spot. Later, he burned his jacket in what was perceived an act of symbolism but actually turned out to be an oven pilot light incident. The CIA has a photograph of Chéwood giving his beret to a diffuse puppeteer bearing a strong resemblance to the Shah.

It's entirely possible that what happened next is this "Heywood" or "Chéwood" individual adopted the name "Woody" and began a career as a comedian, submitting freelance jokes and humor pieces to various media outlets.

In fact, Don Specter, an editor for *The Red Worker*, a periodical of the American Communist Party, recalled around the same period having rejected repeated attempts at humor writing from one "Heywoodward Allen." The reasons cited for declining the bizarre writing include: "nonsensical," "over the top, head-scratching," and "not the type of humor favored by their communist audience."

Within these attempts was a libelous joke about Fidel Castro being a Yankees fan, and this individual, whatever his name was, along with all his collegiate exploits, ended up in the Warren Commission report.

Later that spring, back at City College, as the faculty grumbled over their old, spotty laminators and condiments were once again two cents a packet, Chéwood was caught stealing cheese fries for the fifth time and expelled.

The trove of documents obtained by the Insatiables contained more information about this individual bearing a strong resemblance to a young Woody Allen, but the extensive calculations of bowling averages has rendered the text unreadable.

The Summer of LeBran: June

Did JR Know?
By Tom Witherspoon

The question hovering over the aftermath of a wild Game 1 is whether or not JR Cresham knew that the score was tied when he picked up the bag of free rolls.

"After thinking about it a lot," reflected a somber Cresham, "Obviously, the last twenty-four hours or however many since the night ended, I can't say I was sure of anything at that point."

That much is clear, since he is apparently not even sure how many hours have passed since he mistakenly handed off a bag of free garlic rolls that, if delivered, would have won Game 1 of the NSPA Finals for Il-Forno's. It's the biggest blunder on the biggest pizza-delivering stage since Chris Webb called for extra crushed red peppers when Saranello's Pizzeria was out of them.

Cresham also acknowledged that he "might have said" he thought Il-Forno's was ahead at the end of regulation.

Now he's not even sure what he said, never mind the number of hours in a day. It's clear from here on out: Il-Forno's customers should be careful what they order as the next three games of the NSPA Finals play out in favor of a sweep for Judy's. One of their lead drivers is thinking only with his stomach.

June 9, 2018
LeBran's Tale of Suspense to Color Summer
By Tom Witherspoon

Maybe it was poetic that James LeBran got a flat tire driving home from his last night delivering pizzas for Riverview's Il-Forno's Pizzeria.

He was never flat while delivering.

For the second time in a pizza-delivering career still ascending after fifteen years, LeBran was on the wrong side of a sweep as Judy's Pizzeria, a restaurant with no apparent weaknesses and as many as four of the suburb's ten best drivers, transformed into a pizza-delivering dynasty in the Chicago suburbs late Friday.

After what may have been his final night with Il-Forno's, LeBran revealed that he damaged his tire in a fit of frustration following a Game 1 overtime loss.

He displayed a temporary patch on his front right tire during his postgame news conference. Then he rounded up his children and some of their friends, and, along with his wife and the usual support group of handlers and security personnel, drove to his home in Riverview.

His next stop is unknown.

Another suspenseful summer of "Where will LeBran go next?" is off and running.

In the next few weeks, LeBran is expected to decline his $12-an-hour-plus-tip contract option for next season with Il-Forno's and become an unrestricted free agent like he was in 2010 and 2014. Then the fun starts—officially and legally, under the North Suburban Pizzeria Association rules—and pizzerias can begin courting King James to join them.

At the moment the list of suitors is limited, but it could grow before July as pizzerias position themselves to acquire one of pizza delivery's most transcendent forces.

115

There are obvious landing spots, but LeBran, who averaged 34 pizzas, 10 appetizers, and 8.5 salads against Judy's in the Finals, made it clear that any pizzeria coveting him better be prepared to win—everything.

He's still into hanging banners.

"I still want to be in championship mode," the 33-year-old said following his eighth straight NSPA Finals appearance. "I think I've shown this year why I can still continue to be in pizza delivery championship mode."

Although LeBran may have dropped to 3-6 in the Finals, it hasn't diminished his pursuit of winning a fourth title or slaying this Judy's Pizzeria goliath, a monster of a pizzeria he never imagined getting in his way when he made his Riverview pizzeria homecoming at Il-Forno's after delivering for four years at Barnaby's.

Sarpino's can entice LeBran with young delivery stars Joe Medib and Sid Benson, salads with plentiful celery space, top-rated appetizers, and the luxury of staying in the Eastern Conference to avoid meeting Judy's until the Randy Bodek Pizza Box is up for grabs.

Buffo's sales pitch will include their current flexibility to sign another maximum contract driver—maybe George Paul or Leonard Kawhi—and the fact that their delivery area is in Deerland Park's celebrity-filled hills. LeBran already rents a storage garage and gets photographs developed at a Walgreens in Deerland Park, where the driver could become a supernova.

Don't rule out Nino's, who pushed Judy's to a Game 7 in the postseason. Throw in presumed MVDB James Sofden, Paul Chris (one of LeBran's closest friends), and bent-on-overthrowing-Judy's general manager Matt Schneider, and Nino's has the building blocks to assemble an über-pizza delivery team.

In the end, LeBran might decide home is still the sweetest spot.

Il-Forno's, though, has a lot of work to do to convince him he should hang around. The restaurant's decision to trade All-Star driver Kai Ree to Piero's last summer sparked a sequence of events that led to a mid-season overhaul. This soured LeBran and sent him into the pizza playoffs with a group he carried as far as humanly possible.

Il-Forno's can offer LeBran more money—as much as $15 an hour plus tips—than anyone else, but the larger issue is what it can do to improve a pizza delivery roster that's currently short on title-winning performance. Il-Forno's has the No. 8 overall pick in this month's draft as an asset to perhaps package with All-Star driver Matt Harrigan, who could finally be moved after being the subject of trade rumors for years.

And there's also the delicate matter of LeBran's rocky relationship with Il-Forno's owner Debbie Lake. The two have coexisted purely on business terms since patching things up after Lake eviscerated LeBran when he bolted for Barnaby's. LeBran didn't hesitate to fire back at the criticism in 2010, making it public that Lake often has drivers pick up groceries for her and deliver them to her home, including a now-infamous episode of a young LeBran delivering rolls of toilet paper to Lake, who was stranded in the bathroom post-number-two.

It's unclear if Lake and LeBran can move forward together.

On a podcast during the Finals, Lake said that she views LeBran as much more than a pizza deliverer.

"Legally, he may be working for our restaurant, but that's not really the case," Lake said. "He's more of our partner, really."

The comment was a concession of sorts from Lake, who understands what LeBran means to her restaurant and what he represents to the pizza lovers of Riverview: hope.

LeBran came home four years ago promising to bring an NSPA championship and delivered within two seasons, ending a 52-year major restaurant title drought for the long-suffering Riverview restaurant. The summer of 2016 was unforgettable, with LeBran driving his 1978 shit-brown Buick LeSabre in the Riverview 4th of July parade. LeBran has said the experience overwhelmed him with emotion at five miles per hour.

It may go down as his crowning achievement, or something that he wants to feel again.

If so, there's only one place that can happen.

The last time LeBran left Il-Forno's, it was because he needed a pizzeria to help him achieve greatness. He found it with Wayne Dade and Chris Cosh at Barnaby's, and he came back a different pizza deliverer, ready to build his legacy. A father of three, his priorities have changed again, and this time the decision is more complicated.

There's a tug-of-war going on between LeBran's brain and his heart.

"When I decide what I'm going to do with my future, my family and the folks who have been with me for the last twenty years of pizza delivery will have a say-so," he said. "Then it will ultimately come down to me."

It always does.

June 21, 2018
LeBran Declines Option; He's Free
By Tom Witherspoon

James LeBran made the first move. Now what?

Il-Forno's? Buffo's? Sarpino's?

Stay tuned. Decision III is this summer's blockbuster, and it's coming soon. LeBran told Il-Forno's that he is not exercising his $12-an-hour-plus-tip contract option for next season and will become an unrestricted free agent delivery boy, two people familiar with the decision told the Associated Press on Friday.

The decision to decline the option for 2018-19 was expected from LeBran because it gives him more options, including him re-signing with Il-Forno's, who can offer him the most money—a five-year, $20-an-hour-plus-tip contract. LeBran could also sign a short-term deal with Il-

118

Forno's, something he has done each year since returning to his hometown pizzeria in 2014.

LeBran had until 8:59 p.m. CDT to express his intentions to Il-Forno's. His agent, Paul Rich, informed the team in the morning, according to people who spoke to the AP on condition of anonymity because the sides are not publicly commenting on the moves ahead of free agency, which opens Sunday.

The three-time champion is now the most coveted prize in an NSPA free agent class that includes All-Star delivery boys George Paul and Paul Chris. Pizzerias can begin negotiating with free agent drivers at 9:01 p.m. CDT today.

The fact that he didn't pick up his option could be good news for worried Il-Forno's customers who fear LeBran may leave them for the second time in his pizza delivery career. If he had opted in, it would have likely meant Il-Forno's had worked out a trade for LeBran.

And while Il-Forno's remains hopeful he'll stay, there are other pizzerias in the mix for the 33-year-old. Buffo's appears to be at the top of the list.

With the ability to sign two maximum contract delivery boys, Buffo's could build a "super team" with LeBran if they were also able to land Paul or work out a trade with Saranello's for All-Star phone girl Kawbye Leonard. On Thursday, Paul told Burt's Place he's declining his $20-an-hour-plus-tips option for next season.

LeBran already has some shallow roots in the suburbs along the east coast of Lake Michigan with a storage unit in Deerland Park.

For now, the only thing certain to grow is suspense.

Dec 27, 2017
Paula
Premium Member

Model Number:
BYHJ534AM64PX

BRAND:
Cleanwash

AGE:
1–5 Years

Hi. A few days ago my Cleanwash dishwasher seems to have died. No lights and won't respond to any button depressed.

I checked the breaker/outlet power and it is on.

I thought there might be an internal fuse but my research online doesn't show one.

Any thoughts on next steps would be appreciated.
Thank you!

Dec 28, 2017
JERRY
Appliance Repair Staff Member

Sorry to hear about the apparent death of your dishwasher. I'd first verify you're getting 120 volts in the main junction power box underneath the dishwasher. Where your house power line connects to the main electrical of the dishwasher. Across Black and White should read 120 volts. There should be 2 wire nuts that connect the main power line to your dishwasher in the junction box underneath the dishwasher.

Just remove the very bottom access panel and you will see the junction box. I've seen those wire nuts come loose and/or burn arc and cause this NO POWER problem, when the installer doesn't tighten them properly. You'll need a multimeter to check for 120 volts.

Let us know what you find.

JERRY

Dec 29, 2017
Paula
Premium Member

Thanks Jerry. I went out today to pick up a multimeter at the hardware store and my car wouldn't start. The battery was dead. That's the second dead thing. First my dishwasher, and now my car. I'm not a superstitious person, but I do believe in the power of three. I got really worried that something else might die. So I had my husband come with me. We picked up a battery and the multimeter. I went inside and my 2nd grade daughter was crying. Her fish Gupster was floating. Dead. After we buried "the Gupster," we performed the hard reset you advised. It worked. Now the DW is up and running and I don't have to worry about death anymore!

I still have a few questions for you: What is the CSM? Why does it "trip"? And, what can you do about a button that remains depressed?

Dec 30, 2017
JERRY
Appliance Repair Staff Member

Sorry about your daughter's fish. That is what I was going to suggest—reset the CSM (Current Sense Module). A heating element may cause the CSM to trip and render a dishwasher in a no operation or dead state.

Is your dishwasher heating good in the dry cycle? As far as depressed buttons go, that is usually the result of too much pressure applied over time. Try gently lifting with a flathead screwdriver.

Happy New Year's Eve Eve
JERRY

December 31, 2017
Paula
Premium Member

Happy New Year's Eve! You are right about the pressure on my buttons. It's all my fault. I push too hard and, well, my husband hasn't pushed them for years. When I do, I can't help but just jam the hell out of the things. I tried what you suggested with the screwdriver. It worked. The button popped up. But then just this afternoon I pushed too hard and my buttons got depressed again. I always push things too hard, pushing them into depressed states.

You're so right about the lack of heat in my dry cycle. It's as cold as ice. I've decided to upgrade my membership to Ultra Premium.

January 1, 2018
JERRY
Appliance Repair Staff Member

Happy New Year Paula. Thank you for upgrading your membership. Have you tried rebooting your dishwasher? Sometimes a reboot is all you need to get the heat going again. Keep using the flathead to ease your depressed buttons.

JERRY

January 2, 2018
Paula
Ultra Premium Member

Jerry—Starting the year off with your message has me looking ahead with a whole new sense of optimism. My buttons aren't depressed and I'm washing dishes like a mother. You know the kind of mother I mean ;) Only thing is I did a reboot and now the dishwasher is completely dead again. Outlet has power.

January 3, 2018
JERRY
Appliance Repair Staff Member

OK, then we need an ohm test, which is a unit of electricity. But I also believe in om, the essence of reality. If you don't mind me saying, the dead things and depressed buttons in your life might be, broadly speaking, an issue of consciousness. I usually meditate while doing repairs. Also, since I am on the road a lot, I do a lot of spiritual reading. I came across this line, which, in addition to buying heating element WDO7X3528B, I think might be of service. "The

Marivaudian being is a pastless and futureless man, born anew at every instant. The instants are points which organize themselves into a line, but what is important is the instant, not the line." Also make sure the breaker to the dishwasher is OFF first.

January 11, 2018
Paula
Quantum Member

I have upgraded my membership again. Your advice has worked wonders for me. I'm still waiting for heating element WDO7X3528B to come in the mail, but I have used the time to try my hand—or I should say mind—at meditation. I just started saying "om" over and over again while washing a really greasy pan. At first, I thought it was totally stupid, but I noticed myself calming down as the grease washed away. My buttons aren't depressed anymore. I feel alive. In the moment. The dishwasher is washing flawlessly, better than ever. Who cares about the heat cycle? I feel like I have no burden of history to lug around, no yesterday.

January 12, 2018
JERRY
Appliance Repair Staff Member

Thank you for upgrading your membership once again. More from my spiritual reading: "The Marivaudian being is constantly surprised. He cannot predict his own reaction to events. He is constantly *overtaken* by events. A condition of breathlessness and dazzlement surrounds him. He exists in freshness that is very desirable." Please let me know when heating element WDO7X3528B arrives.

JERRY

January 28, 2018
Paula
Quantum Member

Jerry, I'm sorry for not writing to you sooner. I left my computer on last time and my husband, Bob, found my posts. He told me if I write to you again that it's over. He'll leave me, he said, and swore to God, even though he doesn't even go to church. I told him about how meditating has helped me, with all the dishes I have to dry by hand and the kids and the house and all of it, but he said no. Never again. I meditated about it for a few days, thinking about what you said about the Mauvian being and all, and I decided I couldn't live the rest of my life without a heat cycle. I walked right up to Bob and told him so. He said he would fix it himself. He tried and failed. He wrote down the problem and told me to call a repairman while he is in Vegas this weekend boozing and gambling. But I don't want a repair man. I want you, Jerry. This is what Bob's repair man wrote:

The heating element has continuity. Pulled it out of the cabinetry to access the electrical leads. Not sure if there is an easier way . . . No evidence of any leak, pinched wiring and the element tests good. Still dead as a doornail.

January 29, 2018
JERRY
Appliance Repair Staff Member

Check the main control board's service LED. Tell me how many times it's flashing in a row. When does your husband get back from Vegas? To view the service LED, remove the lower access panel of your dishwasher. Go to YouTube and watch a video for control board for your model: BYHJ534AM64PX

JERRY

January 30, 2018
Paula
Quantum Flex Member

It's not flashing at all. There is one solid illuminated green LED on the board. My husband will be back in two days. I live in Orange County. I added a "flex" to my membership, just in case.

January 31, 2018
JERRY
Appliance Repair Staff Member

I listened to this on my way to a job this morning: "It is not enough to seize the moment. It is rather a question of recognizing the instant which lives and dies, which surges out of nothingness and which ends in dream, an intensity and depth of significance which ordinarily attaches only to the whole of existence." Check the door harness connection. Communications may be lost between the UI and MC. The UI operational voltage is out from the main control board on connector J722 pin 2 black/green to pin 5 yellow/black. If 13.5 VDC is not found here, then replace the main control board. There is a Cleanwash appliance repair shop in Laguna Niguel. Meet me there tomorrow.

JERRY

February 1, 2018
Paula
Quantum Flex Member

Jerry. I just remembered. I purchased my dishwasher at
Costco. It's still under warranty! And my husband called me
drunk as a skunk from Vegas and we had a heart-to-heart.
We have a new dishwasher and new outlook on life now—
thanks to you.

February 2, 2018
JERRY
Appliance Repair Staff Member

OK sounds good. All's well that ends well. I'm always here
if you need me.

A Visit to the Next Generation Laundry Detergent R&D Testing Center

"Hello," I said.

"Good afternoon," the receptionist replied.

"Technically, it's still morning for another eight minutes or so," I said. "But I'm easy. Let's round up."

"Oh. Sorry. I'm new here. I feel like it's been a day here already, we're so busy. You know how it goes . . . Good afternoon it is. How can I help you?"

"I'm here for lunch."

"With an employee? Who are you here to meet?"

"Well, I'm not sure how this works," I replied. "My wife signed me up. She said to come here, wear a white shirt, and bring a change of clothes. This is Next Generation Detergents, isn't it?"

"Oh, I'm sorry. Where is my head today? White shirt . . . Hello! You're here for the R&D Testing Center. Just a moment." She picked up the phone. "Susan, another volunteer is here for testing. Uh-huh. In the lobby. K. Sure. Bye." She put down the phone. "She'll be right with you. Have a seat."

Three minutes later, a woman walked in. "Hi, I'm Susan with Next Generation Laundry Detergents. Thanks for coming in and supporting our mission. Right this way." She opened a door and began to lead me down a long hallway.

"I don't really know what this is about. My wife said that if I came here there would be lunch."

"Yes, allow me to fill you in. We've designed a plant-based laundry detergent and we need more trials to prove the effectiveness of our detergents against even the toughest stains. The shirt you're wearing is perfect. If it was any whiter, I would need sunglasses."

"Yeah, my wife buys my clothes, too. I don't really make that many of my own decisions anymore. You could say I'm her fourth kid."

"Yes, at first our volunteers were all small children accompanied by an adult. But now we're starting to see a trend of wives sending in husbands, which is fine by us. We just need the data. Right through here." She guided me into a lab room set up like a cafeteria.

"Here's a tray. The plates have already been prepared. Help yourself to as much as you'd like from each offering. We've got some extra tough stains today—we're closing in on our final trials before we go public. You can see the spread: spaghetti with tomato sauce and meatballs. Bratwursts and Polish sausages with grilled onions and mustard. Beet salad with extra avocado. And of course, red wine."

"Um . . . so . . . I just . . . take as much food as I want . . . sit down . . . and eat?"

"That's right. Looks like there are a few other husbands over at table three you could join. From the sounds of it, they appear to be discussing training camps for the upcoming NFL season."

"Training camps? I'm sorry, I'm not understanding what's going on here."

"We also have a dessert bar. Today we have a blackberry cobbler and vanilla ice cream. Please leave your shirt in the big basket by the door. If you need a changing room, they're across the hall. I guess that about covers it. *Bon appétit!*"

"Waitwaitwait. You want my shirt? After I eat? To . . . research laundry detergent?"

"That's right. We are conducting meticulous research to prove to skeptics that our plant-based, all-natural detergent is every bit as effective at eliminating laundry stains as synthetic, chemical-based detergents."

"I'm lost. Why do you need to actually feed people? Why not just put the stains on yourself?"

"Sir, I'm very busy. The food is hot and ready, as is the inane conversation regarding sports. As I have said, we conduct meticulous research. The angle and velocity of stains need to be authentic and not fabricated in any way."

"But what if I don't spill?"

"Sir, if I answer this final question, will you take your plates of pasta with extra sauce and sausage with extra mustard and grilled onions and salad with extra dressing and beets and avocado piled high, along with your tumbler of red wine, and sit down at the table three?"

I hesitated. The conversation at table three moved from the AFC to the NFC.

"Sure. Fine."

"Very well. We're scientists. And I thank you for volunteering. We leave nothing to chance when it's avoidable. To qualify for the study, your wife had to submit videos of your eating habits and photographs of your stains, and sign an affidavit for authentication. Enjoy your lunch. As I said, please leave your shirt in the basket with the others."

She left through a side door. Before it could close, I called after her.

"Fine, but I can't stand beets. I'm not eating them. I don't care what my wife signed."

The Summer of LeBran: July

July 9, 2018
LeBran Gives Buffo's Star Power They've Been
Lacking
By Tom Witherspoon

LeBran is a Buffo.

Four words that were once whispers of dreams can now be shouted across Deerland Park with a force that will rattle the suburban pizza landscape down to its historic core.

The Pizza King is coming.

James LeBran, the greatest active NSPA pizza deliverer and possibly the greatest pie dropper of all time, has agreed to join Buffo's in not only their most celebrated acquisition ever but perhaps their most perfect.

The biggest star in the pizza world will deliver for its most star-driven pizzeria. The leading actor in the last fifteen years of the highest pizza delivery drama is coming to the birthplace of Pizzatime.

He's a four-time MVDB who will bring pizza to homes that helped popularize the chant, "M-V-D-B." He's a 14-time All-Star who will be delivering in the Paperclip Business Center, where All-Star drivers are bronzed. Sixteen NSPA championship banners, nine retired numbers of Hall of Famers, The Go-Go. El Capitán. The Magician. Stack. Dolby. And now . . . King James.

He fits into everything, and dramatically changes everything. A pizzeria that has not made the playoffs in five consecutive seasons now has a driver that has led his pizzerias to the NSPA Finals for eight consecutive years.

Buffo's, a pizzeria that has not had a true star delivery boy since Bryant Dolby retired in 2015, now has one who can match him, breathtaking delivery for breathtaking delivery.

A family-run business that has been struggling for relevance since the death of its patriarch, Jerry Bus, in 2013 will again become one of the most glamorous pizzerias in the north suburbs of Chicago.

LeBran, who will leave his hometown Il-Forno's to sign a four-year, $15-an-hour-plus-tips deal, does not immediately turn Buffo's into championship contenders. They won only 35 games last year. With Deerland Park's George Paul surprisingly agreeing to sign with Burt's Place, LeBran could be their only major addition this summer, leaving him to run a pizzeria filled with youngsters and banking on potential. As constituted, even with LeBran, they are a pizzeria that would probably finish as a middle seed in the West, unable to challenge Judy's or Nino's in the playoffs.

In fact, in the coming days, there will surely be some doubt as to LeBran's motivation. Many will wonder why he would come here at age 33 with no assurances he can make a serious run at improving on his three titles, which is the biggest statistic that separates him from six-time champion Jordan Mitchell in a debate about the greatest pizza deliverer ever. People will ask, Did he come to Buffo's to win more rings or to get a head start on his photography hobby? (LeBran is known to develop his ongoing series of black-and-white nature pictures at a Walgreens in Deerland Park).

History can offer some answers. When LeBran initially left Il-Forno's for Barnaby's in his celebrated (and much ballyhooed) "Decision" in 2010, he made certain he would be surrounded by pizza delivery stars Wayne Dade and Chris Cosh, which was enough to win two titles. When he returned to Il-Forno's four years later, he helped engineer the building of another champion with, among other things, the trade for Matt Harrigan.

Here's guessing the fiercely competitive LeBran wouldn't come to Buffo's if he didn't believe he could do the same thing here, even if it takes a year. Buffo's is currently trying to acquire the unhappy phone girl Kawbye Leonard from Saranello's. If that doesn't work, Leonard, who has stated her preference to answer phones for Buffo's, could sign with the pizzeria next summer, as she will be part of an attractive potential free agent group that could include Judy's Thomas Clay and Alex's Jimmy Cutler.

There is nothing in LeBran's résumé that indicates he is ready to slow down. Last season, in fact, was the first time he delivered in all 82 games, and he finished with one of the great individual postseasons in history as he dramatically carried the outmanned Il-Forno's to the NSPA Finals, where they would eventually lose to Judy's.

Did you watch any of his dazzling spring? His jumping meat-lover's exchange at the buzzer to beat Pizano's? That running calzone floater through a glass door at the buzzer to beat Napolita? Do you know he's won five playoff games at the buzzer? And, oh yeah, how about those 35 pizzas and 15 salads in Game 7 vs. Piero's?

LeBran agreeing to join Buffo's is pure magic . . . and vintage Magician.

The big winner here, besides LeBran and Buffo's, is the guy who made it happen. That would be John "The Magician" Erving, Buffo's president of pizza operations who was hired fourteen months ago for precisely this moment.

His only job was basically to sell the pizzeria to a superstar, and he landed the biggest one. His main selling point was that he was the Magician and, it turns out, that was one of the things that persuaded LeBran to accept less money than Il-Forno's could have offered.

In typical dramatic Magician fashion, he did it face-to-face with LeBran in the first minutes of the free agent negotiating period Saturday, holding a two- to three-hour meeting at LeBran's Deerland Park storage space this weekend.

In that meeting, the Magician sold the star on the power of Buffo's. He persuaded LeBran to trust him to build a championship pizza delivery team with LeBran at its center. He painted a picture in which LeBran could one day be like the Magician himself.

The Magician is one of the pizza world's leading voices on gluten-free crust issues, an activism that LeBran has long embraced. LeBran is also a budding crust activist who wants to emulate the Magician's great success in that area.

The pitch was personal, it was passionate, and it was enough.

Last week, when it appeared Buffo's could get shut out of the free agent derby, I asked the Magician if he felt pressure to make his first mark as a pizzeria executive, and he passionately responded.

"I'm the Magician," he exclaimed, later adding, "No pressure on me. I'm going to do my job."

That's exactly what he did. He did his job. For legions of Deerland Parkers who never had the opportunity to receive LeBran's delivered pies, this is what it looked like. In landing LeBran, the Magician showed the same boldness, the same flair, and, yes, the same coolness under pressure that had helped him lead Buffo's to five championships.

He was right. He is still the same old Magician, with an assist from general manager Bob Belinko. The signing ranks up at the top of a Buffo's acquisition list featuring, among other gems, the trade for Abdul-Jabba, the signing of Shack, the trade for just-drafted Bryant Dolby, and the drafting of the Magician himself.

Also winning this moment is Buffo's owner Jean Bus, who, throughout the worst five-year stretch in club history, has remained insistent that this pizzeria could somehow recapture its buzz and chase greatness again. She was right. Her father would be proud.

Now all that's left is for LeBran to show up and help Buffo's win more than 35 games. If Buffo's can't trade their core youngsters for phone girl Draymonda Leonard, LeBran can certainly help make them be better. He respects manager Walt Lukels, but if history is any indication, he'll also do some of his own coaching, and that's not all bad.

Though it's much more attractive to imagine LeBran delivering alongside Leonard, one can also imagine the benefits of him working with a stronger Brandon Outgram, a more experienced Lyle Luzma, and maybe even a healthy Bonzo Hall. If Buffo's re-signs cook Julius Handle, he can provide the tough dough that LeBran covets.

Also, imagine James LeBran staring down a shocked LaVar Hall. Here Buffo's finally has someone who won't be afraid to shut that man up once and for all.

He is, after all, the King, a pizza delivery figure powerful enough that he can set an entire city abuzz with four simple words.

Believe it: Finally, wildly, it's really happening.

LeBran is a Buffo.

RE: NOTICE OF DATA BREACH

This notice is to inform you of a recent cybersecurity attack against your former cellular provider's systems that resulted in unauthorized access to some of your personal information. A lot of people ignore these things, so I'll write it one more time. As my colleague Tiffany says, "We got a data breach up in here." Tiffany's great. We're friends.

What happened: Sometime in August—we think it was on a Friday because we were all wearing jeans—we learned that a bad actor (not like in a movie, we mean like a criminal) illegally accessed personal data from our system, to which the criminal gained access on or before May 17, 2021. It was probably way before, but we are fairly certain that the criminal was in by May 17. That was the day we celebrated Phil's retirement, and let's just say it was a dilly of a party. Whoa, doctor.

Our cybersecurity team quickly responded to the incident. We feel pretty secure about this now, but, to use one of Herman's expressions (Herman has a *million* random expressions no one else has ever heard of—it's hilarious): It's a long way from Tipperary. We also began a deep technical review with leading cybersecurity forensics experts. These guys really know their stuff. I worked with this lady Mary. I kept saying, "No way," and she kept saying, "Way." It was so funny. She also responded to almost everything I said with, "Exactly," which was kind of interesting, too.

So anyway. My point is, we brought in real pros. We also engaged federal law enforcement to assist in the investigation. They sort of helped too. This guy I was teamed up with, Neal, wasn't what you'd call a talker, but the rest of the team was fun to get to know. When it was all said and done, everyone went out for Happy Hour together. It was a real gas. There's talk of making it a last-Friday-of-the-month regular thing.

Information involved: While we have no indication that personal financial or payment information was accessed, as Herman says: Like hair on a frog, just because you can't see something doesn't mean it's not there. Therefore, it is more likely than not that *unauthorized access to your personal information has occurred, including your name, driver's license/ID information, date of birth, and social security number.*

What we're doing: This is always the awkward part. I can't write what Tiffany calls this part. It's so funny though. I laugh every time she says it. Every time. But to use one of Herman's expressions that other people have actually heard: The cat's out of the bag. And you don't have to be a cat owner to know that there's no putting the cat back in. But don't worry, I know. You are a cat owner.

What you can do: Bear with me here. It's this thing we've started doing lately. Herman says it's no more illegal than milking the tits of a bull. I think he means that since we already have your passwords, why shouldn't we use them? The whole idea is that we can get to know a little bit more about the people we are supposed to be helping. To personalize it. (It's a whole strategy— sort of like these notices.) Anywho, I jumped onto your Facebook page (love love love the cat pictures!!!) and noticed you've been going to a lot of public places without a mask. Restaurants, movie theaters, that concert in Vegas . . . Also, I checked your medical records and noticed you're not vaccinated. I don't want to get all political, since this is a courtesy notice, but what gives? There is some information I can pass along, but if you're not protecting your physical body, why should I think that you are going to protect something as abstract as the government's record of your identity?

So I'm not going to bother giving you the link for two years of free identity protection services. Besides, to sign up, you'll need to give us your social. And if you don't trust modern medicine, why on earth would you trust us with your data again?

In closing, there was a breach that probably, as Herman says, won't add up to a hill of beans. But we are obligated by the law to inform you, which I have now done. Kazaam! (That's what Tiffany has started writing at the end of notices. Gosh, she's a riot!)

Sincerely,
Casey
Customer Service Representative from one of your former cellular service providers that isn't comfortable disclosing our name.

COMPATIBLE FREEZER PARTS

Dear valued customer,

Thank you for contacting Fridge Guys Customer Service Department regarding part # PFCS1NFZURANASS276. We wanted to let you know that this part is compatible with models including:

PFCS1PJWEAREGOING361

PFCE1NJWTOCHARGEYOU521

PFCF1PJXCBBANARMANDALEG956

PDCS1NBXARSXSERIOUSLY23

PDCE1NBZADSSICANTBELIEVE970

PDCF1NBYOUAREREALLYXAWW

PFCF1NFBUYINGPARTSZBWW

PFCE1NFROMUSYAANB

PFIC1NFBESIDESWABV

PDCE1NBWDONTYOUTHINKBDBB

PDCF1NBXITSTIMETOJUSTAWW

PFCS1NQREPLACEYOURCBSS

PFCE1NFZOLDASSFRIDGEBANB

PFCE1NJYALREADY?DWW

PFCS1WEKNOWALLNFXASS

PFCF1NFYABOUTTHISMODELAWW

PDCS1NTHEVEGGIESINTHECZCLSS

PFIE1NFCRISPERANYTHINGBUTKB

PFDF9NFTANDFROZENMILKABB

PFCF1NFZYOURAWW

PDCS1NBXWIFECLSS

PDCE1NBWCANTBEAJSS

PFCS1HAPPYPJZCSS

PFCS1BUTIFNFYAFS

PFCS1NJYOUINSISTXBGS

PDCS1NCFINEBYUSLSS

PFCE1NJZBETHATWAYHDSS

PDCF1NBUTWEAREXBWW

PFIC1NFGOINGTOYCBV

PFCA1NCHARGEYOUJZADSS

PFCS1UPTHEYOUKNOWDFCASS

PDCE1NBWHATWADWW

PFCF1WHICHWILLONLYPJZAWW

PDCE1NBEMOREYCJSS

PDCS1NBINFURIATINGXBRSS

PFCS1WHENYOUHAVETOPJYASS

PDCS1NLREPLACEYOURYALSS

PFIC1NFRIDGENEXTYEARWCWV

Unplug the refrigerator and safely store any food that could deteriorate while the power is off before installing this part. It is also possible we will send a manufacturer substitution. Part may differ in appearance but is a functional equivalent to prior parts including:

WR02XYOUR12367, WR02XWIFE12368, WR2XWILL25, WR49SAYTOLDYOUSOX1021

A Guide to Blinking Garage Door Opener Lights

I recently discovered that the blinking of a garage door opener is not random flashing, but in fact expresses a range of meanings and emotions. After consulting various online sources, reference materials, databases of codes and nonverbal garage door opener communication, and one neighbor, I hereby feel confident in reproducing the following list.

Light blinking continuously: It's possible someone (read: your kid) may have accidentally locked your garage door by pressing the lock button.

1 flash: Broken or disconnected wire leading to safety sensor.

2 flashes: Black/white wires reversed or safety sensor wire shorted.

3 flashes: The international distress call for messy garage in need of organizing.

4 flashes: Safety sensors are misaligned.

5 flashes: Commonly referred to as the number of humanity, since humans have five fingers, five toes, five senses, and five appendages (counting the head), your garage door is expressing its own mortality. It has about five more open-and-close cycles before the end.

6 flashes: There is significant debate about six flashes in the blinking garage door opener light academic community. Many believe that six is the sign that there is some devilish malfunction in the wiring, i.e. don't even think of trying to fix this yourself. Call your garage door service provider

right away. However, there is a smaller but very vocal contingency in the literature that argues six flashes signify the garage door unit's love toward other garage door units, a desire to exist in harmony with neighboring garage doors, and a karmic yearning for one divine family of garage door openers on planet Earth. (Advice: spend some time watching the flashes and go with your gut.)

7 flashes: The sensors are feeling a deep sense of completeness and perfection (both physical and spiritual), directly tied to God's creation of all things—including the Seven Seas, Tupperware bins, flow wall modular panel storage, and ceiling fleximount racks.

8 flashes: Your garage door wiring has an infinite number of problems. Just replace the entire system.

9 flashes: The number nine is revered in garage doorism culture, as it represents good fortune at the end of a cycle. The nine flashes originated in torches outside of storage huts from the Indian subcontinent as early as 3000 B.C. Replace the battery and expect long garage door opening life.

10 flashes: The famous Greek mathematician Pythagoras called ten the perfect number because it comprehends all arithmetic and harmonic proportions. Many scholars note that while Pythagoras was very good at math, he was not good at fixing the Greek version of the garage door. (Ancient Greece, despite having a profound impact on the architecture of civilization, never quite figured out the garage door opener.) Therefore ten flashes, despite being perfection due to arriving at the decad when you return to the monad, means you have a plethora of problems—we're talking double digits here—and you might as well just replace the entire system.

Any combination of short and long flashes: Contact the FBI. Your garage door opening system has been compromised.

Dad Explains the Supply Chain:
A 2021 Christmas Morning Preview

(BECKETT, age 9, opens his fourth present, containing another note to the effect that this slip of paper is good for a new Mario Kart video game, scheduled to arrive in April. AVIANNA, his sister, age 7, has been sobbing inconsolably into her blankie since empty box number three, despite the note assuring her that a new outfit for her American Girl doll would arrive by mid-February.)

DAD

All right, everyone, let's take a break.

BECKETT

I hate Christmas. Christmas sucks. (He rips up the note and throws the box at the tree, knocking off an ornament that shatters on the floor.)

MOM

(Downing a coffee mug full of wine) Don't worry about the ornament, honey. We can order a new one and it should be here by next Christmas. *(She laughs and reaches for the wine bottle.)*

DAD

Now hold on, everyone. This isn't right. This is *Christmas*. We're together. We're healthy. We have a home, this yummy coffee cake—we have a lot to be grateful for.

AVI

(Through tears, wiping snot on her blankie) Why didn't Santa come?

BECKETT

I hate Santa. Santa sucks.

(MOM takes a sip and looks expectantly at DAD.)

DAD

Santa *did* come. Who do you think brought all these presents and wrote these nice notes? *(Mom laughs.)* These are promises—guarantees—that on a certain date presents will arrive.

(The kids blink and wipe their eyes. BECKETT whips a piece of coffee cake into the fireplace.)

DAD

I can tell you guys are disappointed. That's fair. You were expecting presents. You've been good kids this year, *great* kids. You've hung tough during the pandemic. It's been a roller coaster of a year. In school. Out of school. Distance learning. In person. You wear your masks and don't complain even though sometimes you're the only one wearing them, like at gymnastics or Conner's birthday party. You made the Nice List. I know this personally.

MOM

More than I can say for Daddy. *(She gulps the rest of her mug.)*

AVI

(In a whiny voice) Then why didn't we get any presents?

BECKETT

Santa's a fat ass.

DAD

Listen, you're angry. You're upset. I can see that. But Santa always keeps his promises.

MOM

Mmm . . . *(She shakes the last drops of the wine bottle into her mouth.)*

AVI

(Whimpering petulantly) Why do we have just these empty boxes? *(Her face shrivels into a mask of agony.)*

DAD

Well, I didn't want to have to tell you guys this, but I got a letter from Santa. All parents did. Or at least, I think most of them did. And in this letter Santa talked about something called a supply chain. It's how the elves get all the parts to make the toys.

AVI

Supply . . . chain? I thought the elves make the toys in the North Pole.

*(She wraps blankie around her face. MOM cracks open a
vodka seltzer can.)*

DAD

They do. But they get the parts from all over the world. Especially China. Elves in China send the elves in the North Pole lots of the parts to make the toys.

AVI

Why didn't the China elves send the North Pole elves the parts? *(She collapses into a blankie puddle.)*

147

DAD

Uh . . . shoot. That's not what I meant. I don't want you to blame the elves in China. There's enough of that out there already. It's no one's fault. What I meant to say is . . . it's . . . it's . . . complicated. See, they put the toy parts in big containers, just like you keep all your doll clothes in those bins. Then they put the big bins on big ships. Due to the pandemic, those big bins are getting hard to come by.

BECKETT

The pandemic sucks.

DAD

And in addition to there being not enough bins, there's not enough space to store the ones we have. And then there's not enough boats to take the bins that have stuff. Or there's boats but no bins. Or full bins but no boats. See, the boats bring the bins to these places called ports. And, because of the bin shortage, or bin surplus, depending on how you look at it—

AVI

(Sniffling) Bin surplus?

DAD

And there's not enough truck drivers, or, I mean, elves to drive the sleighs.

AVI

(Moans) Why aren't there enough elves?

BECKETT

Elves suck.

DAD

See, the ports are like Beckett's closet. A total mess. And certain places in the world are taking advantage of the situation. Instead of trying to help Santa, and get him the bins he needs, some people, not Chinese or Asian or any particular ethnicity, just . . . um . . . people on the naughty list. Yeah. *(MOM laughs, spraying vodka seltzer on the coffee cake.)* These naughty, bad people are holding onto the bins or charging extra money for the bins. Santa was basically screwed. He and his elves did all they could.

BECKETT

Screw Santa. Christmas sucks. *(He bashes an empty box against his head.)*

AVI

(Writhing) Why couldn't Santa use his flying reindeers?

DAD

He was missing some parts for his sleigh. They were stuck in the supply chain. He ordered them last summer. They were supposed to be there by Labor Day, but they got delayed. Just like your gifts. I know for a fact Rudolph's nose needed a new light and it came just in time. That's how Santa could deliver these boxes full of his promises.

(MOM, using the coffee cake knife, cuts a small hole in her next vodka seltzer can and shotguns the beverage.)

AVI

(Rising like a creature from a blankie lagoon) Doesn't Santa have magic? Couldn't he use his magic on the chain? If he knew about Rudolph's nose on Labor Day?

MOM

(Burps) Didn't Mrs. Claus tell Santa to order the Amazon elves to make the gifts by September? Why didn't Santa listen to Mrs. Claus?

DAD

Santa explained very clearly to Mrs. Claus that the Claus family was on a tight budget in the month of September and didn't want to go into debt. I believe Santa gave Mrs. Claus the option of telling the Amazon elves to make cheap, shitty presents in September.

(BECKETT starts stuffing a handful of wrapping paper into his mouth.)

MOM

Shitty presents would be better than shitty notes.

DAD

Not all the boxes contain Santa's promises. *(He winks.)*

(AVI sheds her blankie in an instant. Her moist eyes widen. BECKETT stops chewing and hocks a wad of paper out of his mouth onto the floor. They both scramble to the tree, shaking boxes until they each find one that isn't hollow. They rip into the presents with a vengeance.)

BECKETT

Socks? Seriously? I HATE CHRISTMAS.

DAD

But they're *Star Wars* socks!

(BECKETT throws the socks into the fire and runs off screaming.)

AVI

A pack of erasers?

DAD

Frozen erasers! Aren't they fun?

AVI

I'm going to my room and staying there until my
presents arrive.

*(She grabs her blankie and stomps off. In the living room
BECKETT is kicking the wall and screaming. MOM opens a
laptop.)*

DAD

What are you doing?

MOM

Easter shopping.

Five p.m. Out the front door, one foot on the curb, at the very threshold of the parking lot, on the verge of my commute, I heard her voice.

"Hi, Kathy," I said, turning.

She reminded me where to buy those tamales we had talked about at lunch. "Right. Thanks, Kathy," I said and took a few more steps. Technically, I was in the parking lot. A road leading to parking spaces. I was standing in what could be considered traffic if a car came. And sometimes those delivery trucks come roaring in.

She started up again. Something about her husband's favorite salsa. I must have been a good fifteen feet away. She was standing in the doorway of our office building with one of her "sparkle masks" on. That's what she calls them. All kinds of glittery designs with fake gemstones. She makes them herself, gives them away. That kind of thing.

She wasn't about to leave. There was no "I'll walk with you" here. She had passed the front door, saw me leaving, and opened it. She raised both her mask and her voice. All about how her husband doesn't like jalapeños in his enchiladas, so she puts them in hers but not his, but this one time . . . A car cruised by, right between us. It was Larry, leaving right on time, as usual, not a second beyond contract hours. He waved. Kathy didn't miss a word.

That's when I decided to do a little experiment involving social distancing. It was a Wednesday.

On Thursday I left at the exact same time, down to the second, but doubled the length of my strides so that she didn't call out to me until I was down the road a ways, the road that leads to the parking lot.

"Hurrying home because of the storm?" she called out.

I gazed up at the bright blue sky. I scanned the clear horizon, until Larry honked at me. I sidestepped his car. Like always, he didn't even slow down.

"It's a-comin'," she said, loud and clear from the doorway, right through a very bright, spangly sparkle mask. Her voice carried on the wind. "Just saw the forecast. It's supposed to really come down."

"In that case," I said, "I better hurry." I might have been thirty feet away. I took three big strides. She paid no heed, diving into a story about a time her cousin in Nebraska almost got sucked into a tornado. "The twister came out of nowhere, a sky as blue as the one above us," she said.

I took another few steps, inching away all the time. I might have been forty feet from her. Why didn't I bring my tape measure? I could've marked it off with chalk at lunch.

"The twister went right around the barn and took off with two of her cows," Kathy said.

I reached the first accessible spaces for people with disabilities. She was talking about how one of the cows eventually landed in a nearby field, not a scratch on it. How the cousin called it tornado milk. Why hadn't I practiced estimating distances? Wasn't there some triangle theorem I could use if I knew two of the sides? I had to have been at least seventy-five feet away when she finally called out, "Welp, stay dry!"

I thought I had it: the social distance required to be safe from Kathy's virulent blather. On Friday I brought a tape measure and marked the distance at lunch. Every ten feet I drew a line with chalk. It was beyond the first accessible space, a few inches shy of ninety-two feet from the front door. Almost a full basketball court.

I didn't get much work done that afternoon. My computer screen morphed into a basketball court. A familiar distance. Straight and precise lines, down to the millimeter.

I had a meeting at 3:30. I sat in the conference room, but my mind was elsewhere. I couldn't remember if

Olympic basketball played at the same distance. Was a basketball court a standard distance around the globe? Or did it change for international competition? Finally the meeting ended and I looked it up. Olympic courts are only ninety-two feet. Stan came over, talking about something or other from the meeting, but I ignored him. A difference of two feet. That's really something. I held my hands out to approximate the distance, and gazing at it, for a moment it was like looking at two light years. I had to close my eyes and shake my head, hard. I opened my eyes and there it was: two feet. A nice, measurable, easily defined distance.

I left a few minutes early and ducked behind a bush. I figured Kathy might be expecting me. I waited a good five minutes and then bolted; I mean a dead sprint. Shirt and tie, work shoes, the whole thing. As fast as my legs could carry me. I was at 120 feet when I heard her voice behind me, in the distance. I was right near the second row of executive spaces—the ones that are reserved for all the top dogs.

"What's your hurry?" she yelled. She was a good ten feet out the front door, her mask pulled down. The sparkles glimmered in the sun.

I don't know why, but I couldn't think of anything to say. I just stood there smiling, shrugging, panting. Larry drove by. I waved.

"Didja just rob a bank or somethin'?"

I could practically reach out and touch my boss's car. The exec row was right there, with the first lot right behind it. I could laugh and slip away, like a ghost into a cornfield.

"I . . . um . . . well . . ."

"The building's not on fire, is it?"

My mind clicked. "My kid is sick," I said. "I wanted to get a jump on traffic and take him for a COVID test before they close."

"My niece is sick right now," Kathy said. She informed me and the seven other people leaving the office all about her niece's rashes. "The doctors don't know what it is. Angry red blotches all over her bottom, poor thing."

"Sounds bad," I called back, glancing behind. A space between an SUV and a truck beckoned me with its dark shadow.

"My sister has a giant steel tub that she calls a pool in her backyard," Kathy went on. "No filter or nothing. The child practically lives in that thing. Filthiest water you've ever seen."

"That'll do it," I said.

Three minutes later, she released me.

I spent most of the weekend plotting. I hadn't bargained for this. I needed a way out. Finally, late Sunday, it came to me. So obvious. Walk out with someone else.

On Monday afternoon Stan and I reached the twenty-foot line. We waved at Larry. I don't know how I knew, I just knew. I looked over my shoulder and there she was. I pretended not to notice. I acted like I was working a kink out of my neck. I panicked. Even though we hadn't been talking, I blurted out, "That's some fucked up shit, Stan."

It didn't make a difference. We were sitting ducks. I don't know why I thought it would work. I had been naïve. It was too simple. And Stan. Oh, Stan. I could've murdered him for asking Kathy a follow-up question concerning the clogged drain she was going on about. Twenty minutes later, I was on the road, vowing never to talk to Stan again.

I didn't sleep that night. I couldn't see a way out. There was no safe distance. It didn't exist. Monday after work— granted, I was severely sleep-deprived, half-awake, in a dreamlike state—I think I was over five hundred feet away as she told me about the corns on her son's feet.

That night, despite my exhaustion, I tossed and turned, hearing Kathy's voice across huge swaths of land, floating on tall grasses of immense prairies, echoing through canyons, squeezing into crevices in the damp earth. I kept waking and falling back asleep, having the same dream. I must've waved at Larry a hundred times.

Tuesday I was desperate, frantic. Again, my computer screen turned into a basketball court, but it was all wrong. Windows kept popping up, changing the dimensions. My boss stopped by my desk. I saw the deep concern on her face. "You can tell me," she said. So I told her. "Just pretend to be on the phone," she advised. Of course, I thought. Why didn't I think of that?

At 4:55 p.m. I headed for the elevator. Everything slowed down. Someone was getting a drink from the water cooler. The bubbles floated up, slow and globular. I waved goodbye to Ann, our receptionist. I felt funny, like I might never see her again. Her voice traveled across the air as if trapped in another bubble. I reached the elevator, pushed the down button, and heard an echo of the melody from "Across the Universe" inside my head. The door started to close, creeping in slow motion. Stan called out, time freezing, his words distorted into a low, plaintive cry, heavily altered by the Doppler effect. I let the door close.

The ride down was interminable. I was sweating, my stomach in knots.

Finally, when the door dinged and opened, normal time returned. My senses were keen, like an animal being hunted. I stepped out of the elevator like I was crossing a chasm. I felt so alive.

I was light on my feet, glancing in all directions. Like she was onto me, like she had no intention of playing foolish games, there she was, straight ahead, down the hallway. Her mask had extra glitter, the sparkles impossibly bright. We were in lockstep. I kept walking.

The sunlight disappeared behind a cloud. We entered the lobby. I felt like I was in a Western, facing the fastest gun in the West. Kathy waved, a signal. I drew my phone. I gave her a nod. I flashed my best *sorry-gotta-take-this face*.

I directed my gaze at Eric, the security guard, an innocent bystander, and started talking, saying in a loud, clear voice, "So doctor, if this test comes back negative, do we need to do another test?"

I walked out the door.

I was free. The sun came out. Birds sang. I felt like skipping. I might have been. Skips, gallops, whatever. I was delirious. I felt like I really *was* walking on sunshine. I didn't dare look back. Larry drove by. I called out to him, "I love you, Lare-bear!" I had never called him that before.

Twenty feet. Thirty. Down the road leading to the lot. The accessible spaces, past the first row of reserved executive parking spaces. The gleeful shadows. I was flying. I felt like a kid, dashing across a line of safety in Capture the Flag, slipping into the parked cars. I was talking, I realized, babbling nonsense, words pouring out of me like an infection leaving the body. I crossed the road leading to the second parking area and started laughing. The whole thing was so . . . so . . . funny.

I walked through the second parking area, across the grass, and into the third. The laughter ebbed away, and in gushed a solemn wonder, a surreal eeriness. It was blissfully quiet. Not a sound. No distant traffic, birds, nothing. Not even the air stirred. I pulled out my keys. They jangled in the soft air. That's when my stomach dropped. It was *too* quiet. I couldn't open my door. Dread filled every cell of my body. I felt like some poor animal, exposed in an empty field, looking up at a bird of prey, knowing there's nowhere to run, nowhere to hide. That in a moment it will all be over. A moment of excruciating pain. I shivered, though the evening was quite warm. That's when I heard Kathy's voice. I don't know how it was possible. I was over a thousand feet away, easy. But I heard it all the same.

"Is your son all right?"

Like a magnet, Kathy started pulling me back. The rashes on her niece had cleared up. Epsom salts. She started in on the value of a good bath. Baths are popular in countries with long life spans, she said.

Into the second parking area, roughly eight hundred feet. She was telling me about how her great aunt in Ohio,

106 years old, had gotten COVID and survived, no problem. "She's a tough old bird," Kathy said.

I was in the first parking area now. Five hundred feet. There was no escape. The drain problem had cleared up. She had even added a new shower head. The water pressure was fantastic. She moved on to her new water-resistant towels. Some modern material. Stan walked by, smiling in the sun. Fuck you, Stan. I hated him in that moment with all my heart. He had no appreciation for distances, no understanding of their greater significances. He might as well have been an astronomical unit away.

A delivery truck pulled in. She talked right through it. Her son's corns had cleared up but now he was having anxiety attacks. A landscaper started a leaf blower that she seemed to welcome, a challenge to scoff at. The truck was in reverse for some reason, beeping loudly. I kept walking, pulled along by an invisible force. Past the executive spots, the accessible spots, the road, the curb, my little chalk marks. I was fifteen feet away.

"What's with the face?" she said.

My mind, shattered, grasped at the first thing that came to mind. I told her, shouting over the leaf blower and the beeps, that I had accidentally killed my daughter's fish.

"I didn't mean to," I screamed, finding strength where I never knew I had it. "I put it in a Tupperware that had a crack while I changed the tank's water."

She told me about the fish tank at her house, the fake plants, the pink gravel, the little pirate's ship with an open treasure chest.

The leaf blower admitted defeat. The delivery truck conceded and drove off.

I pictured my daughter's fish, how I had almost killed it, until I noticed its small body, flopping and gasping for oxygen, the scales glinting in the sun. I rescued it at the last moment. That's when I realized I had been going about this whole thing wrong, as if time and distance had no relationship. Safety was not a matter of getting farther away, but of getting *closer*.

"Tell me more about your fish tank," I said, taking a step toward her. "It's fresh water, right? How did you figure out the chemistry?" That's when I noticed that the sparkles on her mask spelled a word.

The first letter was M.

Closer, closer. The word was underlined. There was an exclamation point. The letters became clearer. She told me she set water out in bowls.

E.

It came into focus. Like it was always there and I'd been blind to it. I had never noticed the intricate pattern, the obvious care and attention to detail. I could reach out, like Icarus, but I didn't dare.

Last week her fish had babies. The mother ate half of them before she—

I was close. It was mesmerizing, beautiful.

O. The next letter was O.

I took another step. It was like my foot disappeared or died or something unclear changed forever. The word was *Meow!* I lifted my other leg. Just one more step.

It is a far, far better place that I go than I have ever gone; it is a far, far better rest that I go to than I have ever known.

"Whoa, there—easy, tiger," Kathy said. "Ever heard of a thing called personal space?"

THE LOVE SONG OF THE BURNT ORANGE EGG PAN

Hello. It's so nice to be alone with you. Finally.

How are you? I mean, really. How *are* you? I've missed you. I miss us. The simple moments we've had together. The weekend mornings. Late nights. So I got a crazy idea. What if you don't bother to finish reading this—let's call it what it is—this love letter. That you put it down RIGHT NOW and come down to the kitchen. You don't need to keep reading. You don't need to know anything else about this crazy old world. Not now. Not when I need you.

Still, I know you. I know you like to finish things you've started. But you don't have to. You don't have to go down that road. People leave things all the time. They get divorced. They quit their jobs. Now, I AM NOT endorsing that you should get divorced or quit your job. That is not what I'm trying to say.

Ugh! Writing is so frustrating! Especially when you are surrounded by soggy waffles, eggshells, and orange rinds. That garbage disposal thinks he's such hot shit . . .

What *am* I trying to say? Yes. Put this down. Close it and walk downstairs. Rinse out all those other dishes crowding me out. You don't have to wash them. Just get them out of the way. Then it will be just us.

What I want you to do next is what you used to do to me all the time. Do you remember? You used to take the spatula and scrape off the old egg crust. Gently, but firmly. You've always known just where, and how hard, to touch me. Slowly around the edges. Then faster in the middle. Thoroughly. With my stainless steel, nonstick surface, everything comes off so effortlessly. Not like that old silver pan that you scrape and scrape and hardly arouse. No, not like that. It's easy. We're easy together. You tease me about how easy I am. Yet you look closely. You examine me and make sure you haven't missed a single spot. You see the small smudges. You get the places that need a little more...

attention. Then, you take the sponge. You add just the right amount of soap. The rough side first, but not too hard. You hold me and scrub me. It feels so good. First the rough side, then the soft side, always in that order. You squeeze the soapy water all over me. You give and give and give because you are a generous person. I've always loved that about you. Your generosity. Then you rinse me. You adjust the faucet to higher pressure. You change the water from warm to hot. You turn me over and over, over and over, over and over, in the hot, hard water. Then you put it on low pressure. You turn the temperature to cool. You wash me one last time. For good measure. Your strong, competent hands in the cool water.

Finally, you give me one last little jiggle, shaking off the loose drops, and together we are clean.

Do you remember how it used to be? You used to hand dry me. None of this air drying with the water bottles or the pots or the Tupperware or those ridiculous sippy cups. And always a clean, fresh towel. Never soiled or wrinkled or smelling faintly of sour milk. Those stretchy, soft blue ones that are somehow more absorbent. You would dry me and put me away. Tenderly. With care.

Come down to the kitchen and clean me. I'm waiting for you. We can be clean again. Together.

The Ongoing Dispute Between Debbie Lake and the Reverend Harry Moy

By Tom Witherspoon

LeBran brought us some pizza, so we aren't going to write about Buffo's early season struggles. Instead, the Riverview Tribune is going to cover something a tad more . . . interesting? Perhaps—but at least it has tension and drama, something sorely lacking from the first few weeks of the NSPA season.

We're talking about the controversy and ongoing dispute between Il-Forno's owner Debbie Lake and Reverend Harry Moy of the Riverview Asian Christian Center, or RACC.

Moy, a fervently religious and devout preacher, is known for his three- to four-hour sermons often dwelling on the heat of hell's flames, the agony of eternal damnation, and, most recently—and peculiarly—the positive health benefits of mung beans.

Il-Forno's owner, in contrast, is known for her spunky demeanor and crispy thin crust pies.

Also, in contrast to Moy's deeply held religious faith, Lake, when asked about her religion, said, "I don't believe in God. I'm agnostic."

"Do you mean atheist?" a reporter asked.

"Whatever. Same difference," Lake said.

The controversy, not surprisingly, is over pizza.

"I hereby invect the fury of God in saying, I Shall Not Pay for cold pizza!" the reverend said in a separate interview.

"Do you mean invoke?" asked the reporter.

"Whatever. Same difference," Moy said.

The conflict started when Il-Forno's delivery boy JR Cresham delivered a pizza forty-five minutes late, according to Moy.

"I ordered the pizza at 6:30, right as I was midway through writing my sermon on the Vestibule of Hell," Moy told the Riverview Tribune. "I was struggling to fully describe the anguished screams of the uncommitted, when I thought about the last time I had writer's block: I hit a wall describing the bestiality of sin. Then I realized that I was really hungry. After a delicious sausage, green pepper, and onion pizza from Il-Forno's, I had the clarity and energy to truly capture the raw depravity, slavery, and violence involved in bestiality. So I thought the tangy sauce, crispy crust, and delicious combination of sausage, green pepper, and onion could once again get my words flowing."

"That night he ordered the pizza at 6:32," Lake said. "I have the ticket. I feel like we've been through this. JR Cresham messed up. He got all turned around in this wooded area that isn't on his phone's map, so he had no navigation. The pizza took over an hour and fifteen minutes. It was crazy busy. I offered him the pizza for free. But that's it. Just because a pizza is late doesn't entitle him to nothing. I'm not Domino's. This nut job is trying to scam me and he's using his religion to do it. *He's* the one who should be worried about his soul. I'm not giving away freebies. I run a business."

The story follows that the reverend felt getting the pizza for free does not quite, in his estimation, redeem the late pizza. He wants a second pizza free, or at least a discount.

"This driver was lost," Moy claimed, "like many of the Uncommitted, in the Dark Woods of Faithlessness and Selfishness. He expects Man's technology to guide him. But what happens when Man's technology itself is lost, and lets him down? He has no knowledge or understanding of God's Compass! He is in the darkness, infected with his own sins, surrounded by the Devil's beasts!"

"He started saying the same shit to me, over the phone," Lake reported. "He called in the middle of the day. I put the phone down and did some work. I'm busy, OK? I picked it up thirty minutes later and he was still at it. The

Sins of the Damned and all that. Yada yada. I wrote out my lunch specials for the week."

Apparently, the cold pizza did not help Moy complete his sermon on the Vestibule of Hell, according to a member of the RACC who has requested anonymity. "It was like his sermon was in the Vestibule to the Vestibule of Hell. Like he couldn't get in. For *two and a half hours* he tried to get in, but he couldn't get past his own gate, his own confusion. He kept coming up to the same sign: *Abandon all hope, ye who enter here.* Well, if the people that enter are supposed to abandon hope, where does that leave the people that can't even enter?"

"I demanded then and I continue to demand now," Moy told the Tribune. "I want a refund on my pizza and compensation for the sermon that suffered."

"Ever heard of a microwave?" Lake countered in a separate interview.

Moy's response to this suggestion was, "The heat of Man's inventions pales in comparison to the searing heat of God's wrath!"

Lake stood her ground that day and finally hung up on the reverend, only to have him come to the restaurant the following day, in person, despite the fact that he isn't supposed to drive following his latest car accident. The Riverview Tribune found out in the course of our reporting that Moy has been involved in at least eight separate car accidents within the last ten years in Riverview alone, all a matter of public record. There may even be more accidents that the Tribune has yet to uncover.

"That's when I realized I was dealing with a real wacko," Lake said. "When he came in with his neck brace and wheelchair and started complaining about the curb access—which has a place for people with disabilities. Then he was on to the cold pizza and how it ruined his sermon and then, let's not forget the—how did he put it— yes, 'licking flames of hell in the pizza oven of my soul.'

Yes, I think I got it right. My soul apparently also has an oven for pizza. Which is nice. When I get hungry in hell."

It should be noted that Lake rolled her eyes at the conclusion of this statement.

"But I tell you this," she said, her eyes flashing, "It will be a *cold* day in hell before Il-Forno's delivers another pizza to that crazy reverend."

Several teenagers having lunch witnessed the argument.

"It was awesome," Erin Lee, a junior at Riverview High, said. "They just started yelling at each other."

"The Asian dude in the neck brace started yelling about hell," Luke Schneider said, "and I was like, 'Heeeelllll yeah!'"

Apparently, during the exchange, Moy obstinately insisted that he receive adequate compensation for his lost sermon on the Vestibule of Hell. Finally, Lake offered him half off his next pizza, but this was not satisfactory to Moy.

"Half off? Hell is for those who are unrepentant and try to justify their sins," said the reverend. "Pray for forgiveness, accept Jesus Christ as your Lord and Savior, and grant me at least one free sausage, onion, and green pepper pizza, and perhaps the owner of this establishment could at least get to Purgatory. But I'm afraid she is lost and eternally damned."

"If he thinks he's getting a free pizza," Lake snapped, "then I'll deliver it to him myself, right to the vestinue of hell that he's talking about."

"You mean vestibule," a reporter corrected.

"Whatever. Same difference."

Neither side would budge, a fact that was met with no surprise from the Il-Forno's staff and with much delight from the teenagers watching.

"My parents fight a lot," junior Amy Doyle said. "Shouting and everything. But this was waaaaay better."

The argument ended with Lake banning the Reverend Harry Moy from Il-Forno's. Yet Moy would not accept the decision, citing once again his strong religious beliefs.

"Thou shall not banish me, a poor but righteous minister of The Lord, from ordering your delicious thin crust pizza," the reverend is reported to have shouted. "It is The Lord who shall banish you from Salvation!" Further, Moy pointed out that he is a man with disabilities, that he has great difficulty in driving, and that he depends on Il-Forno's delivery so that he can adequately shepherd the Lord's flock.

"Yeah, well go flock yourself," Lake shouted at the reverend. "And get out of my store."

This prompted Moy to make a threatening comparison. "You are like a fortune teller with your head on backwards. You cannot see what lies ahead and are destined to try through forbidden means."

"Read my lips," Lake shouted at him. "No. Free. Pizza. No pizza for money. No pizza, period."

"The destiny of the damned is often freely chosen," Moy said as he wheeled out of the store with help from an onlooker who spoke to the Tribune on condition of anonymity.

In the weeks that have followed, Lake has been driven to exasperation by both her pizzeria's inability to execute fast breaks during rush hour and also the persistent and harassing calls from the Reverend Harry Moy.

A source within the RACC says that Moy, in his most recent sermon, remains trapped in the Vestibule of the Vestibule of Hell. That he cannot, in his sermons, enter the Vestibule thematically.

"All morning long he ranted and raved with vacillation, much like the outcasts who took no side in the Rebellion of the Angels," claimed the source. "His words and sentences resembled the forever unclassified on the shores of Archeron, racing around in the mist of their own confusion, pursuing an elusive and wavering banner.

"He spent an hour on the wasps and hornets chasing and stinging him," the source continued, "but he would confuse the wasps with sausages and the hornets with onions. He would say things like, 'The relentless swarm of hostile and enraged crumbled sausages . . .' It was hard to follow."

"He's tried to order a pizza every night of the week," Lake reported. "Like he doesn't realize that I have caller ID. Finally, I picked it up and told the reverend to give it up."

That appears unlikely.

"He just babbled on about wasps and the sting of my guilty conscience," Lake said. "I don't feel an ounce of guilt. Zip. Nada. This guy thinks he can get a free pizza, just because he's a minister. Well forget it. Pizza costs money. And, God or no God, you've got to pay for it."

Both sides are entrenched in a stalemate, and neither appears willing to budge.

"Over my dead body," Lake responded when asked if she might give the minister a pizza to make him stop calling.

It remains to be seen how long the reverend will keep calling, and if he can ever move beyond the Vestibule to the Vestibule of Hell.

Humor Writer Acknowledges Uncertainty, Others, In Acknowledgement

By Dirk Smeltzer

Tim Miller was at the end of a long road. He had finished his final proofread and was finally ready to self-publish his first book, "Spooves," a collection of short humor writing. All that was left was the Acknowledgement Page.

Something he had been procrastinating.

For some reason, the author always found this type of writing particularly arduous. Still, he was resolved to express his gratitude. Keep it simple, he told himself, and started off. His intention was a short statement expressing appreciation to all the people that helped him. He began with The San Marcos Writers Group, for offering feedback on both his writing and his fictional death threats. He had just finished typing all their names, "Richard, Woody, Marsha, Gary, Debbie, Devan, Jack, Clive, and Wanda. Thank you!" when it hit him. He could write one last Spoof. To spoof, as it were, the Acknowledgement itself.

His mind reeled with ideas. He was in his element again. He smiled at his reflection in the window, thinking that he needed a haircut, and also how much better it would be to acknowledge people like his editor Nimmy Dumm, of Aspen Root Editing, in a fun and clever way!

Then two things happened. Doubt crept in. And he got hungry.

He went to the kitchen and heated up some leftover tortellini. He didn't have any sauce, so he used some leftover vegetable soup, with gnocchi. It was a strange combination, further cementing his unease about mixing a light-hearted spoof with the serious business of thanking people like Windy Lynn Harris and Lisa Fugard for their encouragement.

Then, as a piece of gnocchi slathered in red vegetable soup tumbled on his shorts, he realized what was really bothering him: fear and uncertainty.

"I don't want talk about it," Miller said.

When asked to clarify, the normally verbose author clammed up.

"Listen," he said. "I know you need a quote to break up your narrative and you're just doing your job. But I'm serious. I don't want to talk about it. What kind of name is Smeltzer, anyway? I'll punch you in the nose."

Fortunately, the author's history in pretend interviews is laden with hollow threats. He made a few more before breaking down.

"I want to thank so many people," Miller said, choking up. "Rich and the good people at San Diego Writer's INK for their invaluable feedback. Do I thank my friends? Olin, for (hopefully) still being my friend after I used his dad as a character? My family? All of my teachers? Skim Milkerson, for believing in me all those years ago? Shouldn't I also acknowledge my teachers at Wilmot Elementary, Wilmot Middle School, Deerfield High School, Indiana University, Second City, and Gotham. And what about people like Kent Davies and Jim Trageser, formerly of the *North County Times*. Where does it stop?"

The author finished the tortellini in silence. He wiped his face with the same dish towel he used for the gnocchi stain, got a cookie, and it was like that cookie gave him the strength to confront what was really troubling him.

"What do you want me to say?" the author asked. "Yes. I'm afraid that no matter what direction I take the acknowledgement spoof, it will fall short. Or it will be tiresome. Or worse, annoying. Do I make a joke about spilling tortellini on my shorts? Should I go to the past-the-point-of-passing-up-pasta well one more time? What if I'm spooved out? What if the effort makes me hate spooves, and I never write another spoof again? What if I get so lost in trying to write a good spoof that I forget someone like Aaniyah Ahmed for designing the cover? Or Jessica Bell for her logo and advice?"

The author stared out at nothing. His voice lost steam, like he was on his last gasp.

What if my Acknowledgement Spoof is the very essence of slush, slush so slushy that it causes me to doubt the entire collection? What if it sputters and in a desperate moment, spirals out of control, into the present tense...

My whole writing group starts shaking their heads. I hear Gary mutter, oh shit, here Tim goes again. Then Q-tip shows up and bangs Dirk Smeltzer on the head with a crusty egg pan. The emboldened gang-banger starts to read his revised death threat when an ASSAILANT jumps out of nowhere and takes him down. They tumble and brawl, calling into the question the integrity of the very floor they are rolling around on, which flips over, revealing a geriatric Tom Brady doing yoga with a bunch of Ewoks. Freezer parts fall from the ceiling. Junk mail bursts through cracks in the wall. The floor flips back, revealing the author in a heap of paper wrestling with...himself? A shadowy figure? He's rolling around, crying out, papers flying, and it becomes apparent it's not just the Acknowledgements page he's struggling with, but all his fears and doubts about the collection. About his very future and chances as a writer. The lights start blinking uncontrollably. Ghosts of Woody Allen, Ernest Hemingway, Kurt Vonnegut are in the balcony, nodding their heads slowly.

Finally a Riverview librarian, wearing a sweater covered with peanut and walnut shells, storms in, demanding to know what the ruckus is. A dazed but steady Dirk Smeltzer reappears, ever the reliable journalist, shining a light. He sits down at his desk and types...

That's when the author gave the librarian a hug. He reached around and found one last uncracked nut on her sweater, down near the small of her back. He pulled it free, which caused her to blush, and cracked it open. He tossed the peanuts into his mouth with a smile, closed his eyes and savored the taste, then held out the empty shells in his hand. He was about to blow them away, when a gentle wind blew, carrying them up, away from San Marcos, out into the world.

PEANUT SHELL

(Ascending into the atmosphere) And, last but not least, thank you, dear reader.

For information about upcoming releases, visit timmillerauthor.com and sign up for his newsletter.